Lovers Like You and I

Minakshi Thakur's first book, *An Indian Evening*, a collection of poems in English, was published by Writers Workshop in 2002. She has since published two collections of Hindi poems: *Jab Utthi Yavanika* (2003); and *Neend Ka Akhiri Pul* (2010), which was shortlisted for the Sahitya Akademi Yuva Puraskar 2012. In the same year, she was awarded the Sangam House Fellowship, an international writers' residency in Bengaluru. Minakshi has trained in Khayal and Dhrupad and enjoys singing. This is her first novel.

Lovers Like You and I

MINAKSHI THAKUR

HarperCollins *Publishers* India

First published in 2013 by
HarperCollins *Publishers* India

Building 10, Tower A, 4th Floor, DLF Cyber City, Phase II,
Gurugram Haryana – 122002, India
www.harpercollins.co.in

ISBN: 978-93-5116-029-8

2 4 6 8 10 9 7 5 3 1

Typeset in 11/15 Dante MT
by Jojy Philip, New Delhi 110 015

Printed and bound at
MicroPrints India, New Delhi

For booklovers,
Pisima and Bidhu Bhaiya

To Nayan, over a hot mug of Irish coffee

Jugnu died. Pregnant. Unwed and unhappy. She hung herself from the fan after an argument with her mum.

She couldn't let anyone harm the child. She had nightmares about the ad signage down the road from her house, lurid neon boards stalking her, clawing at her, shouting MTP.

So she chose to kill herself.

Jugnu still looked lovely, lying on a long slab of ice in the sitting room. Her fair skin pallid now, she lay peacefully, sleeping eyelids hiding her brilliant cat-like green eyes. The beautiful, errant and impulsive Jugnu was no more. Deepesh, her lover, sat sobbing by her side.

That night, Nayan dreamt of Jugnu. 'Life is strange, Nayan,' she said. 'Death will be stranger still. Someday, I shall tell you over a mug of Irish coffee.' Nayan had woken up and stood

staring out of her window at Jugnu's room in the house opposite hers. She thought of their little game of communicating by switching on and off the yellow lights in their rooms.

She half-expected Jugnu to appear at her window any moment and switch the lights in her room off and on, twice, meaning, 'What? Are you sleepless? Insomnia, hmm?'

Nayan walked restlessly up and down the chequered floor of her room for a long time. Their game of lights had come to a standstill. Her neighbour, her childhood friend, two years her senior in school, whose notebooks carried the name Jagpreet Singh would not come back from the dead. Jugnu of the firefly eyes was very far way.

Three months later, when the sensation of Jugnu's suicide had worn off and the women in the neighbourhood had stopped discussing it over kitty parties, Jugnu's mother, Mrs Singh, summoned Nayan to give her an envelope. She had found it lying in Jugnu's closet and kept it hidden for fear of stumbling upon another secret of her dead daughter's life. The sealed envelope was dated 4 August 1988 – the day Jugnu ceased to be – and it read: 'To Nayan, over a hot mug of Irish coffee!'

Nayan unfolded the letter and began reading.

4 August 1988

Nayan,

Life is strange. Death will be stranger still. I wish I could tell you about it, share the experience with you – speaking to you from the other side of this life.

I am three months and twelve days pregnant today. I've kept count of each day since the doctor first told me about it. Have been marking my calendar in the same way as we used to cross dates with felt pens long before our New Year picnic actually arrived. They were times of innocent anticipation, each moment of waiting a small universe eager to be born.

Those years have passed by, Nayan. Life is no more a glass, crystal clear. No more that old gin bottle we used to fill with tiny fish or tadpoles (we could never tell one from the other!) from that dirty little pond on our Chhattarpur farm. Life seems to have forgotten innocence. It seems to have made a remote memory of everything… everything I thought carried meaning and breathed a soul into it. Small but precious things like love and spirit. Love, I thought, was always giving, its generosity boundless. But what it is taking from me today makes me wonder what love really is all about, and how many faces it has. The bottle of gin has fogged up and become murky with anguish.

They are ashamed. Ma, Deepesh, Deepesh's mother. I'm not. I'm anxious. Heartbroken. In fact, I began to die the minute I saw their eyes change, the colours of calm leave their faces. Something inside me died just then, and kept dying. I wanted to let you know I was leaving, but you wouldn't let me go if I told you so.

Somebody is listening to *Madhushala* nearby. Must be Kullu uncle. Only he loves music enough to hear Manna

De sing at this hour. The ambience is just right for it; candles dripping into shapeless lumps of wax in every house at load-shedding and the clouds preparing to pour after midnight. In this dimly lit, languid hour, the music is deliciously intoxicating.

Chhote se jeevan mein kitna
pyaar karoon, pee lun haala

(How much can I love or drink
in this brief life of mine)

...swagat ke hi saath vida ki
hoti dekhi tayyiyari
band lagi hone khulte hi
meri jeevan madhushala

(I saw them prepare for a farewell
alongside the welcome,
the tavern of my life began
to close down as soon as it opened)

I feel grateful to Kullu uncle. And thank you for everything. It's only close to death that one begins to see and feel grateful for the endless possibilities of living, for the manifold could-have-beens.

You will get this letter after I'm gone. I can see candles flicker in your house. In my mind, I walk to your house and come back numberless times, after ruffling your hair, talking with you and sharing your evening snack.

I can feel another life quiver with premonition inside me. Maybe this little ball of hopelessness in my tummy has an inkling already. A sense of foreboding, I guess. Remember how Madam Mary Ann would take vocab and diction lessons with all the senior classes together? Remember how we used to say 'foreboding' as in fore-bo-ding, meaning premonition, and pre-mo-ni-tion meaning what? Fore-bo-ding!

It is difficult to cut the ties, to dissolve all that has been. But, my calendar ends here. My palmistry, whatever little I know of it from Cheiro, says you'll answer the questions I haven't quite answered. Yes, trust me, you have those lines. You'll meet many people, many lovers, some like me, some different. They'll give you all the answers.

Live beautifully,
Jugnu

Jugnu is dead. Her child is dead. Her death has become old news now. From its shock, rises the sweet smell of decay. Her memories, fond or bitter, will gradually gather dust and be forgotten like discarded furniture covered with cobwebs in the attic.

'This is what society does to women who question, women who try to break away, women whom Deepesh's mother calls waifs, truants, profane gypsies,' Jugnu had said after watching a movie adaptation of Bimal Mitra's *Sahib, Bibi aur Ghulam*.

Nayan's eyes ran over the words in the letter a hundred times.

'Can't you do something about your handwriting? It's horrid! I don't feel like looking at your notebooks, Jugnu…'

But the era of shared lives was past. It would be an age of secret lives now.

An age of secret lives

Nayan sat painting her nails with blue ink. She had nothing to do except take a desultory walk from one thought to another. University exams over, she had plenty of free time on her hands, so she followed her mother, Ratri, around to music concerts. Nayan would do this while in school, too: paint her nails with ink during free periods when they would be lucky enough to not have a substitute teacher coming in to mind the minds of sixty girls.

Ma had lovely hands, with shapely nails that strummed the tanpura strings. She used to paint her nails with the latest Lakme shades that flooded the market. But that was some years ago. Now, she left them plain and uncoloured. As a child, Nayan coloured her clipped nails with blue ink, wondering whether someday people would begin to emulate her and it would become a trend, a fashion statement.

Neel, her elder brother, would scold her, 'What strange

things you keep doing with yourself. Just the other day, you painted trees and flowers all over your arms and hands, and now, this. Your nails look repulsive!'

He would never understand fashion. Not just fashion, but her sense of it…

What were Jugnu's nails like? She had flat, brittle ones, pale yellow half-moons. They were called lunulas. They are still called lunulas, although Jugnu who had them is gone. To Nayan's mind everything associated with Jugnu had been transported to another unseen realm the day she died. She took with her everything she owned to the past tense. Nayan wondered how old Jugnu's child would have been today. She calculated on her fingers, adding the number of years the neighbourhood had taken to forget the shame, and the almost endless list of insinuations attached to Jugnu's suicide to three months and twelve days. All those years had failed to efface from her mind even a single word of Jugnu's last letter, the memory of those years when Jugnu had taught her that every empty hour was a lonely hour. But loneliness was one thing Nayan would not trade for anything else. Except love.

Love. Was that it? She felt unsure now. Didn't unrequited love leave one lonelier and bereft? Shouldn't she have known beforehand that Jugnu was going to die, that Jugnu was completely alone and helpless? Had she known, Jugnu would have been alive. Nayan would have saved her.

Three in the afternoon by the grandfather clock, Ghantidas (as Neel and Nayan had christened it years ago). It struck every hour as if to reiterate its presence. The silence in the house stirred up as if from a dreamless slumber, rippled awhile and then settled like water in an urn. It's time for Guruji Maharaj's afternoon riyaz with Ma, and her, if she would join them. She had to. Ma needed her to sing from behind her, and not just sit on the stage and strum the tanpura, swaying her head like a puppet this way and that. Raga Puriya Kalyan shall most ingratiatingly sweep away her emptiness for some time now.

Another thought. Not a passing one this time. Salil. How curious he was to know where the flat notes, the komal swaras of Puriya, glided to the pure notes of Kalyan. Salil was deeply interested in learning the nuances of mixed ragas like Puriya Kalyan, Basant Bahar, Adaana Malhar, Bhairav Kalyan…

Where was he now? What would he be doing today, at this hour, while she sang Puriya Kalyan with Ma and Guruji Maharaj?

'Bhairav takes a detour into Kalyan in the same way as I take a detour from my studio to your college,' Salil had said one day while they were walking from India Gate towards the Gallery of Modern Art. 'It's like the sun walking from dawn towards dusk. Bhairav of the flat Rishabh and sombre Gandhar embraces the sharp Madhyam of graceful Kalyan in a bylane of Mehrauli.'

Salil never moved at a set pace on a straight route in a planned manner. He had no plans for life. No map, no destination, nor any desire or ambition to live a life of luxury. His life meandered as desultorily as Nayan's thoughts at this hour. At twenty-six, he had already taken up, tried, tested and given up on several avenues, which included a civil engineering course from IIT Kanpur, a postgraduate course in medieval history, a photography course in the US, and research in music at Benares Hindu University. He had begun each time with utmost sincerity – he had almost a religious zeal for new beginnings – and showed signs of being wise and perspicacious. But perspectives changed with time and each one of his endeavours failed to give him the contentment and challenge he was looking for.

However, he dreamt endlessly. And he believed in packing up and walking behind his dreams. The year that Nayan met him was the year of his most novel venture. That dingy cubbyhole near Mehrauli, which he liked to call his studio, wherein he played music on his sitar all day, reconstructed artifacts picked up from here and there, carved small sculptures which had no buyers, and wrote ghazals and free verses which never found their way to any periodical anywhere. This studio called 'Anayaas' had happened to him by fluke, hence the name. Life itself was for him a chance happening, a happy accident. And he was struggling in his own leisurely manner to understand what to do with that chance.

Saving art was his latest passion. He had stumbled upon it and Nayan in a similar chance fashion. Neither fell in his orbit really.

What was his orbit anyway?

Serendipity

Khud se hi be-khabar hai ek lamha
Shaam tak dopehar hai ek lamha

They had fought over a new edition of the *Divan-e-Ghalib* released by the Mirza Ghalib Academy on his 195th birth anniversary. It was exquisitely designed, with portraits of the poet by artists from all over India and Pakistan and biographical anecdotes to add to the translations of his verses. There was just one copy of it left at the Shri Ram Centre bookstore.

Nayan and Salil stood vying for it. Nayan had noticed him earlier in the day at a seminar on the relevance of Ghalib's poetry in the twentieth century.

They kept saying: 'I came before, I picked it first...' The bookstore manager suggested he could get another copy in a week's time.

Salil gave it to her then, making a huge show of his generosity

towards her. Then, when she turned to leave, he stopped her and said, 'Will you come with me for a cup of tea?'

Nayan had looked at him incredulously. '*What*?'

'A cup of tea? Just here. That stall round the corner, beside the National School of Drama. A week is too long a time. I want to look at those portraits of Ghalib. *Now*.'

It was Ghalib and not she he desired a teatime tête-à-tête with; the two-rupee chai was simply a paltry bribe. Feeling a little demeaned and not knowing what to say, Nayan had walked across the roundabout to the Bhagwan Das tea stall with him, oblivious of the innumerable strolls that awaited them in the future.

Invisible letters

She stood leaning over the terrace railing, watching cars, buses, three-wheelers, scooters and sleek bikes crawl, wriggle and whizz past the traffic signal. The weather was turning; there was a nip in the air. She could smell Durga puja in the soft breeze that blew through her hair intermittently. October wasn't far away. Ma would soon carry out elaborate preparations for the puja at home. She would also take her to the Kali Bari nearby. Pandals would come up in parks. Although Dashami was big in Bengal, Bihar and Assam, some Bengali colonies in Delhi too made it a grand affair. She went pandal-hopping with Ma to Chittaranjan Park every year. It wasn't too far from where they lived.

She loved October, for the pleasant sunlit afternoons, for the balmy warmth that seemed to stream in and out of every house, for the air perfumed with incense from the aarti for the Goddess. Huge idols of Durga, her neatly chiselled face, her red brocade sari, the majestic lion as her vahaka, a queer amalgam

of chants from the *Durga Saptashati* and the latest Bollywood numbers – the raunchiest ones in particular – would soon fill the days and nights.

Young Bengali girls would wake up in the early hours and move around stealthily, gathering harshringaar flowers from the lawns of neighbouring houses.

Oh, how the harshringaar bloomed at night and fell before light kissed the earth! Their sweet smell that knew no boundaries floated across from the puja room to every nook of the house and outside. It touched Rani, the bai who'd wash clothes and hang them on the line on the roof; Tara, Kullu uncle's son's newly-wed bride who'd step out fresh from the bath and stand before the mirror drying her long black hair; Jugnu's room, which had remained locked for so many years now; and Salil's letters that lay in a wooden casket, the lid of which Nayan opened every night to let in fresh air. Those twenty-seven letters whose words, she thought, would wither and die if she kept them shut all the time in that box.

Nayan too wrote him letters. In invisible ink. With a pen dipped in fresh orange juice. Letters that could be read only when passed over a candle flame.

'Your letters are so delicate, your poetry so fragile that I fear ruining them as I read them over and over again out of greed for more and more of you. I treat them as something alive. I show them the cool moonlight of midnight and the satin first light of the sun at dawn. I fear getting overwhelmed when reading through them, I worry that a careless drop of tear will smudge the ink,' she had written in invisible ink.

Salil had not known the trick. Did he ever get to read the letters then? Maybe.

21 August 1999. It's midnight, says Ghantidas.

You've been walking on the moon tonight,
    I know.
You've been strolling out there tonight,
    I'm certain.
You have been walking up and down,
Sulking about something,
Pondering over some sonnet,
Some unfinished, silly lyric of yours,
Stamping, rubbing your feet
Out of irritability, I know.
'Cause the moon has come down tonight
Hanging from the branch
Of my neem tree,
Cribbing about those aching footmarks
On his shoulders.

17 September 1999. Ten minutes past one in the night by Ghantidas.

The sweet delusion of my soul rises in ecstasy like a bubble in a champagne flute, only to kiss the brim and burst into a union with the fluid twilight within... I can see two gold bands swim towards each other, intertwine, then disengage and chase each other, play and frolic in that sea of intoxication. I can almost touch the momentary exuberance of the mad convergence of my world with yours. That joy, fleeting, yet eternal in its brief permanence, is like the world's last sea wave lapping at my feet and ebbing away.

I feel drunk, drunk on the devastating mirage of an immeasurable, ambiguous emotion – love.

5 October 1999. Two tranquil hours past midnight by Ghantidas.

But love is like poetry. Like verse. And even the blankest of verse has some metre, some rhythm, something to measure it by. The champagne must flow at a patient pace in order to intoxicate and sustain itself in the nerves of those who drink it.

Whoever thought love is a free verse was wrong. Free verse itself was never free. I am teaching myself to love with patience, to love in moderation, in a manner that my love can sustain itself.

12 October 1999. Two loony minutes past three in the night.

Love is insane, but lovers need sanity to make it swim. Or else the wine intoxicates to such a high that it spills over and the madness becomes difficult to contain in the goblet.

20 October 1999. Three dark hours past midnight.

I wish I could trim and throw away memories like I cut my nails and shove them away into a dustbin... That reminds me, I haven't cut my nails in so many days. They almost look like talons now. Do memories grow talons too?

5 November 1999. Swinging to dusk.

It's twenty-eight minutes past five. I am sitting on the jhoola in the terrace. Love Papa for it. It's one of the most wonderful gifts he has given me. The sky has burst into whorls of dappled crimson. Clouds of gold have scattered across that end in the west where the sun's pouring more colours – tangerine, rust and pink. It's preparing to set in some minutes, flashing a brilliant finale, sprinkling vermillion all over the endless expanse. Is there a wedding in the skies tonight?

8 November 1999. Ten minutes of lemon tea after sunset.

Have been sweeping my nerves; red arteries moulded in fire and blue veins borrowed from the sea. I am quite a chimneysweeper when it comes to clearing the recesses of my mind. So, while sweeping this afternoon, I often stopped short. I found couplets of your incomplete verses; a drop of your tear from when you were sozzled on your last birthday; a sketchy picture of our imaginary house with a big terrace overlooking a river; the assuaging four o'clock sunlight we played with every afternoon; my favourite Egyptian strappy sandals, which you broke by forever stamping on them; those often quiet, sometimes peopled roads we walked on like apparitions looking at the moon and counting how far away Poornima, the full moon, was… And your routine question at that: 'Who is Poornima?'… And our silly, routine laughter that followed. Also, that 'Hello!' on the phone at three in the night that would echo through my being.

26 November 1999. An autumn afternoon oblivious of time.

By the unruly clock in my mind, I dream. Images, pictures, voices, shadows, people, stars, history, they all fall like semul flowers from the blazing red trees to the earth. And I sleep on the bed of flowers, thinking and living spring, in grey autumn.

Has the world fallen from that old branch, which shivers in the sad, supple breeze? Has the last flower fallen?

15 December 1999. Seventeen minutes before Ghantidas will strike two back home.

In Kalchini with Ma and grandparents. Fireflies have lit up their hearts. The frogs tell their own stories, singing *tarr-toink, tarr-toink* to insects that play their anklet-like *chun-chun chun-chun* jingle in the backdrop. I hallucinate: Jugnu and I are playing hopscotch in the driveway. Jugnu and I are sitting on the roof making masks for a fancy-dress contest in school. We are peering inside the room where Ma is singing with her tanpura. Jugnu's messing up my palm with red ink, talking with the airs of a palmist. We are buying candles for Diwali in the crowded market behind JNU. Jugnu snatches away the candle I pick, and runs. I run after her but she's out of sight; I have lost her in the maze of the market. And then her mother, Mrs Singh, I hear her scream...

The darkness seems less astounding than usual tonight. It's chilling outside. I shrink in my quilt even though the kerosene lamp by my bedside warms the room a bit. I pray to Kali. My prayer is not a ritual any more, it is a selfish plea – to heal the wounds that wreak havoc tonight.

31 December 1999. Couple of minutes to go before another year begins.

The year is drawing to a close and a new year waits to be born. How close are end and beginning today and how far removed they shall be tomorrow. Three hundred and sixty-four days, twelve months between this 1st and next 31st.

A dance party is on at the Golf Club tonight.

FM is playing Pancham da's *'Phir wohi raat hai...'* I chuckle listening to it. Wonder whether these things, songs, books and other keepsakes, will still remain important to us when we grow older. Will they evoke the same feelings and bring back past associations?

The fire in the grate gradually turns to ashes while fireworks at the club break the dense fog to startle the skies.

23 January 2000. A half-tipsy hour, feverish and orange.

I've been running a fever since afternoon. Have popped an Actifed. I feel intoxicated swinging back and forth on the jhoola, watching the sun melt into nothingness.

10 February 2000. Ghantidas says, 'Bed-tea, sir!'

It has rained out of the blue
and a bright February morning sleeps
quite forgotten in satin covers
as the day gets wet through and through!

16 February 2000. Ghantidas can't be heard. He's revelling in spring song.

Happy notes of Basant Bahar fill the room. Ma is sitting on a mat, her slender fingers strumming the tanpura strings. Pa-Sa-Sa-Sa…Pa-Sa-Sa-Sa…Pa-Sa-Sa-Sa goes the pattern in endless circles. Guruji Maharaj is singing, eyes closed, both hands moving gracefully in the air, moulding, cajoling, caressing notes to comply to the passion of Basant, springtime. He has been living with us for three months now. He has been diagnosed with stage three leukaemia. Which is disintegrating him each day.

For Ma at this hour, there exist just the two of them, guru and shishya, in the sanctum of surs they have built for themselves. She tells me that the possibility of space between Sa and Re, Dha and Ni, any two notes for that matter, is immense once you start exploring the world of music, or jahaan-e-mausiki as Guruji Maharaj refers to it. You begin the alap after closing your eyes and connect with the silence within. One has to seek permission from the silence within oneself before embarking on the journey of a raga. You are a cartographer, a nakshanavees. You have to pray to the shunya in your soul to allow you to begin mapping a raga with your voice. That is why you must sit quiet for a while before beginning the alap.

Guruji Maharaj is on the bandish now: '*Phaguwa braj dekhan ko chalo ri...*' Ma listens to his soulful voice serenade the disease within, appeasing his last muse, it seems. A tiny pearl-drop of a tear glistens beneath her closed eyelids.

28 February 2000. Midnight again.

The moon looks flawless tonight, his reflection shimmering in the pond beneath the rose garden. He smiles and says, 'No complaints, no footmarks!' You haven't been visiting. Why have you stopped writing ghazals?

6 March 2000. Time? Three-thirty, four, four-thirty or maybe five-ish...

The semals are ablaze now; the weather, soft and mellow. I sit on the mosaic floor beside the chik-blinds that filter balmy sunlight into the verandah at the back of my house. Soft light dances on the floor and a broken piece of red bangle embedded in the mosaic glints in it from time to time. I try to visualize the construction worker who must have broken one of the dozen colourful bangles on her hand while fixing mortar for the mosaic flooring. It happens again, the delusion: bangles strewn on the floor... bunches of them hanging from the chiks, romancing the light like the stained glasses in the school chapel windows where Jugnu and I first met Jeeban... Red, blue, green bangles with slight chinks in them... Fragile bangles, dozens and dozens of them, a kaleidoscope of colours...

And that particular piece preserved forever in the tile... What must that woman have been like – she who left a piece of herself preserved in this house for ever?

27 March 2000. Half-hour inside a box of nicotine, past two a.m.

Look, how immensely simple Gulzar saab is.

He writes,

'Yaad hai ik din...
mere mez pe baithe-baithe
cigarette ki dibiya par tumne,
chhote se ik paudhe ka
ek sketch banaya tha
Aakar dekho,
Us paudhe par phool aaya hai!'

(You remember one day
sitting at my desk,
you had sketched a small plant
over my pack of cigarettes?
Come and have a look,
that plant has begun to flower!)

Don't I keep covering your packs with graffiti? *Unpe phool aaye hain kya*? Have those grown flowers yet? No?

Alas, I am ineffectual!

4 April 2000. An hour of thinking before noon. Not of you, the cacti!

Have been sipping the silences of our last meeting at Jeeban's tea party. Did you notice the new cactus he has added to his terrace garden? He's got the most exotic ones I have ever seen. I don't know whether you noticed Meera, the quiet woman on the wheelchair. Meera's been this way for three years now, since a year before she met Jeeban. She's a lovely person. Takes a little time to open up, though. You must see how she paints. I wanted you to talk to her, but you were unusually quiet, magnanimous with words, to my surprise, only when it came to Jeeban's cacti.

Jeeban first met Meera at the inauguration of her first exhibition. You know, Salil, Jeeban, the stubborn, kurta-clad, bearded, live-life-king-size bloke, and Meera, the painter, are due to get married by Diwali this year. Isn't it lovely? They are in love, Jeeban and Meera.

1 March 2001. A shaft of orange happiness in my cup.

We have forgotten that we have to die someday. And in that forgetting, we've locked up our lives somewhere deep inside us. I watch leaves fall from trees all around in the somewhat moody wind. *Bichhte jaa rahe hain patte mere sheher ki raahon mein. Patte-patte par koi chitthi likkhi hai.* There is a letter on every leaf. Letters that wish you happiness. *Tumhare shahar ka haal sunao?* Where and how have you been?

10 June 2001. Does it really matter?

What has become dated? What has ceased to be? Love, or the delusion of it?

6 July 2001. When did you last think of me?

Bhairav and Kalyan do not meet now. You have stopped taking a detour from your complex labyrinth to mine. The bridge between the morning and evening raga has collapsed. But when did the breaking deluge come? The rains have only begun now. Monsoon's here. I have been trying to cajole Ma into singing Miyan ki Malhar. Guruji Maharaj had written this bandish himself: '*Sajan ban mein jhoola lagaao re, jhir-jhir aayi kali badariyan. Sajan, hari-hari chudiyan mangaao re…*'

10 October 2001. Urging my heart to love you more.

It's five minutes to six in the morning. Slept at one, and woke up to Bozo barking furiously around three-thirty. It must have seen a cat, or probably a roving burglar near a gate. It's pleasantly cold outside. I can see a black bird fly across the Qutab in the distance, past the only visible star. No! Venus, the planet. Cannot see the sun yet. Ma will be up in a little while and we shall sing together. Raga Vibhas today… It's been a long time since we sang it. Sometimes, these days, when I sit with Ma for riyaz and close my eyes to follow her as she begins the alap, I feel I'll find you standing before me when we come to the end of the bandish.

The tiny red light on top of the Qutab is shining through the slight mist in air. The mynas and other birds are still snuggled up in their warm nests. A merry bunch of coal-black crows have started clamouring on the eucalyptus branches as a group of early risers marches by towards the colony park for a morning walk. Streetlights are fading slowly and the mad rush hasn't commenced on the roads yet.

What are you doing; wherever you are? Sleeping? In the same pair of frayed jeans, torn at the feet, its edges coming off in threads? Sleeping, turned away from the skylight, soft, caramel morning light falling through it upon the open book near your pillow, reading which you fell asleep last night, your nicotine breath filling the room, and countless cigarette stubs in your self-made, overburdened ashtray?

Jeeban

Jeeban was two years Nayan's senior in school and later in college. Founder of a radical students' street theatre group, president of the college, a trendsetter on the university campus, university topper in economics, everybody expected him to either take the civil services exam or enter politics, given the contacts he had accrued as the college president and an activist of the youth wing of the BJP. Jeeban went on to become a journalist instead.

Nayan met him through Jugnu; Jeeban was in the same class as Jugnu in school and college, and the two of them got along like a house on fire. He introduced Nayan to literature that transcended the barrier of language – poetry beyond British poetry, prose beyond English prose – splashing her mind with names like Rumi, Khusrau, Faiz, Tagore, Jeebanananda Das, Shakti Chattopadhyay, Ginsberg, Akhmatova, Brodsky, Rilke, Szymborska, Jimenez, Nirala, Dostoesvsky, Saramago, Llosa,

Borges, Calvino, and so many more greats. Before him she had known of Mirza Ghalib, the Romantics, and could, of course, recite 'Daffodils' word for word in one breath.

He was the one who taught her to ride a motorbike, though she was rather delicate for his robust Enfield. He introduced her to alcohol in college, taught her to fix a 'mast' stiff drink. She learnt from him that you didn't really need a berth for a good train trip, that the fun lay in the deep and shallow conversations friends had standing all night at the door of the coach. He had a great love for cooking and chess. He was practical, fun, with a fine taste in art and indulgence. He had his life figured out more or less, his aspirations and emotions sorted. He had a short fuse and would often lose his temper. Working with a leading daily in the capital had made him a man about town, but that was a price one had to pay to run the rat race that being part of the media in the nineties increasingly entailed. But he loved what he did – the sanity and street smartness it gave him.

He was someone you could lean on in hard times, and Nayan turned to him whenever crises, big or small, overcame her.

Salil

Salil's letters were actually the ghazals and free verse he wrote. He wrote them anywhere and everywhere, throwing most of them away and pocketing a select few. For some reason, he liked the ones he wrote at the National School of Drama while waiting to see a play, sitting under the sheesham tree that had a sleeping branch hanging at right angles above the head of anyone who sat on the bench under it.

He had his haunts where he would sit alone reading or waiting for ideas to come. He read widely, across disciplines. He had many friends at the Jawaharlal Nehru University who he would spend days and weeks with. They were apparently Marxist in their leanings, but somewhere within they were subconsciously softening in their anti-establishment stance, constantly looking for a more liberal alternative to Marx and Lenin.

Unlike his Qutab friends, Salil did not have any concrete

ideology. He believed his ideology, as also his religion, would come to him on its own. He would find them some day, lying somewhere like unidentified, unclaimed objects, like a landmine perhaps, which would explode when stepped upon. Thereafter, all that was rusting in his mind would be ripped apart to make way for a sparkling new awareness and wisdom. But till that happened, life was a wait, a curious gestation.

Jeeban had said one day, 'Nayan, your friend Salil is a daydreamer. Such vagary will lead him nowhere. A good guy, though – sensitive...very sensitive. He wants to look into the soul of everything that comes his way. Ask him to come over sometime. I like the way he plays his mouth organ on the bus, wholeheartedly, engrossed in himself every time, as if it's the last time he's playing it. You must hear him, Meera. It's your turn, haan. You are taking a lot of time.' This last bit to Meera, asking her to make her move at chess.

'I take a little time because I use my mind, Jeeban,' said Meera.

'Oh! So go on, princess! Meanwhile, let me get myself a small vodka with Limca and a slice of lemon. Anybody interested?'

'No, Jeeban,' Meera and Nayan replied together.

'Get us Limca if you manage to save some after fixing your small vodka,' Meera called out to him, a smile of contentment on the strangely charming pallor of her face.

Raga Marwa, late afternoon

Ratri is practising in the guest room in the south-western portion of the house. She is sitting on an Assamese straw mat. The mat is the only object visible from a distant corner in the garden where Nayan sits alone, not quite listening.

It was a wedding gift from her parents. The hill-like patterns on its sides in red, blue and green have turned faint and its plain straw-coloured body has become tattered but shines in the sun still. The ends sewn up with red cloth have started coming loose too. Nayan's mother loves the mat and used to mend it every six months in the past. But now it is beyond repair. The straw has become brittle with age.

Her mother looks celestial at this moment. Her fingers play Ma-Sa-Sa-Sa...Ma-Sa-Sa-Sa...Ma-Sa-Sa-Sa on the tanpura. Circles of surs ripple through the house. Plaintive notes of Raga Marwa swivel in her voice. Things that lie quiet and forgotten in the house wake up as if on cue from Ratri. Dust motes can

be seen twirling – as though trying to reorder their chaos – to her beat in the spotlight of twilight sun that bathes Ratri and the mat golden.

By her side on the bed lies Guruji Maharaj, eyes closed, ears alert to each note. His silver tray of betel leaves and areca nuts sits by his side, and a spittoon under his bed. Guruji Maharaj, now frail, his white blood cell count beyond control and days diminishing, listens to her every day. He keeps slipping into a semi-comatose state now and then.

Ratri's crisp red handloom sari reflects some of its colour on her face. She is wearing a red vermillion teeka on her forehead. Her hair is tied up in a loose bun with a wooden stick from which dangle three little jasmines, also made of wood. Her ochre-gold profile can be seen in the life-size glass painting of Lord Krishna hanging exactly in line with her shoulders on the wall beside the bed. To Nayan, her mother looks like a shadow, a watercolour portrait of her own self.

Rani, the maid, comes in after starching her mistress's saris, and squats quietly at the door for a while to listen to Ratri with open-mouthed wonder. She cringes away from her own palms that still smell of fresh starch. Then suddenly remembering it's time, she hurries to the kitchen to make ginger tea for Nayan who is lying out on the lawns now, thinking and listening to the strains of vilambit khayal. She imagines her mother being heard far out in the distance, where hundreds of birds clamour, maybe gossiping about the peacocks that will appear in the jungle beyond, soon after sunset, and brazenly croon their cravings.

There's a brown girl in the rain

The rains had flooded Salil's studio. There was ankle-deep water all around, even after Nayan and he had thrown out bucketfuls. The asbestos roof had started to leak. The well-timed patter of water falling drop by drop filled the room. Raindrops hung at the orifices for a fleeting second before hitting the utensils and buckets. Salil had borrowed them from neighbours to place under the leaking holes in the roof. A line of smoky haze rose from the incense stick Nayan had lit to counter the damp smell that had filled the studio.

They sat in one corner of the studio on a slightly raised parapet, huddled close under an umbrella, their shoulders joined, jeans-clad legs folded up and supporting their chins. Two cheap glasses, half-filled with very milky tea from a teastall nearby, stood poised beside them on a tiny, low mud table Salil had made himself.

A Navy Cut cigarette burning between his fingers, Salil

looked at Nayan impishly, singing as he grit his teeth, 'There's a brown girl in the rain…tra la la la'. His smiling gaze moved up and down and round the studio. Nayan chuckled, sipping her tea, even as she tried clamping down the umbrella handle between them.

'So, Mr Poet. All your efforts go waste. Your words are dripping from your studio walls.' Salil had written poems on the walls all over the studio. And now, it was gradually getting smudged in the monsoon that had lasted longer than expected that year.

'Never mind. It's good in a way. The slate lies clean for fresh poems… She looks like the sugar in the plum…plum plum…' he broke into the song again. Then, said:

'Apne seene pe likkhi hai,
jab bhi likkhi hai
tavareekh jala kar,
nayi-naveli nazm koi…'

(I have engraved on my heart
each time I've written
burning down all that is history
a fresh new song…)

Nayan looked out of the barred window. She could see the Qutab Minar through the lattice of grey rain. A wet crow came flying in from somewhere and sat on the window, irritably flapping its wings to splatter water off its body.

'Do you ever see yourself getting married?'

Salil laughed. 'Why do you ask? I don't know. I really don't know. But if I do, it'll have to be by the riverside.'

'Why? Why a river?' Nayan asked.

'So that I can push my wife into the river if I don't like the fact that I'm married and that I can't rove all my life. That's why I'll never get married to you. I won't have the heart to push you into the river... But seriously, I would love to see the reflection of us together, sitting around the sacred agni in the water.'

'Us together by the river...' The words merged with the blood pulsing through her veins. 'And then?'

'Then, my wife and I, we'll make paperboats out of an evening tabloid and set sail on the river together.' Nayan's eyes widened with amazement and Salil laughed out loud. The studio echoed with his transparent laughter and almost made them forget the stolid monotone of the rainwater falling from the roof into the buckets and on their umbrella.

'No, I'm not joking. I will do it. I still do it when I am alone near a stream or a river.'

'Us-together-by-the-river...floating-paperboats-on-the-river...' Nayan felt the words circuit through her blood in a loop like a refrain.

Salil resumed his song, 'There's a brown girl in the rain, tra la la la,' laughing at his own childish fantasies.

'And you are singing the wrong word, Mr Know-it-all,' Nayan complained. 'It's "There's a brown girl in the *ring*", not "rain"!'

'But my girl's in the *rain*,' Salil said, enveloped in the dense rings of cigarette smoke.

'Is there a reason behind everything, Nayan? Do we always say or do things for a reason? Why do I say a "river" when you ask about marriage? The first thing my eyes see is a river and the sacramental fire looking into its fluid mirror.'

'On the surface, yes. Not everything needs to have a meaning. But I believe there is an underlying connection between every incident, every meeting, every person you talk to. Even if you exchange just a few words or a fleeting gesture of the eye. Nothing happens without a reason. All the people who pass you by, the brief crossing of paths and events are part of the cosmic scheme of time and space. No happening is a chance happening.'

'Do you know why you've met me, Nayan?'

'Yes, partly. But I guess time shall unfold the larger purpose.' They looked at each other for a moment and smiled. Salil's eyes watered. They reminded her of some lake by a crumbling, forgotten fort. She had been to such a place, maybe as a child, she remembered vaguely.

'What is it?' Nayan asked.

'Nothing!' he said. Looking into her eyes again, he sang, 'There's a brown girl in the *rain*...'

'Shut up, for God's sake.' They grazed past the question, wandering off to the metronome of the leaking roof.

The wet crow still sat on the windowsill, shaking his head and caw-cawing now and then.

'See, even that crow hates your Egyptian sandals. Look how suspiciously he's looking at them.' Salil laughed, pointing at Nayan's prized pair of camel-coloured sandals that hung from the window latch to dry.

'That crow surely belongs to your clan. That's why he doesn't like my trendy sandals.'

'He doesn't like you much either.'

'That's his problem,' retorted Nayan, a wry smile on her face.

'Which is just as well because I'll break his bones if he happens to.' Salil finished his sentence and stepped down from the parapet. Nayan looked at him while he lit another cigarette and, standing in ankle-deep water, began to scribble away on a damp wall. She stood up too, closing the umbrella. Hitching her jeans further up to her knees, she walked across the waterlog to the window to shoo the crow away.

Ratri

'Your father has become an island,' Ratri said. 'His work has robbed him of time and words, which could comfort us and save us from drifting apart. I can't do much now to bridge the distance between us. But he loves you and Neel. He adores you both. It's just that he is so engrossed in his work he does not remember his way back to us sometimes. Let's just hope he completes this research successfully.'

Nayan sat on the bed listening to her mother. Shadows of the small round mirrors on the red gurjari bedspread danced restlessly on the walls and ceiling of the room. Nayan opened Ratri's casket of gold trinkets and turned it upside down. They added some more glint to the walls. Nayan looked up at the dervishes on the walls. She tried to identify a pattern in their dancing.

'So, when does Papa plan to come down?' she asked her mother. 'It's been four days now. Have you been to his study upstairs?'

The room was dim except for the light from the window by which her mother stood, looking outside. Grey streaks had begun to show up in her hair that flowed down to her waist. Her gaze seemed to be gauging the sunlit haze across the lawn. Beyond the flowerbeds, the bamboos were cooing to each other even as the easterly sauntered through them. Ma looked like a sculpture, a terracotta figurine. She was beautiful, her skin a rare shade that made her appear exquisitely earthy; it was neither fair, nor dusky, but a tinge of red, a sheer but subtle flush, reflecting probably the quiet passion she held for life.

In these moments, she would usually recount tales and incidents, fish out keepsakes for Nayan to see, tell her about her parents, her family and childhood – stories that mattered.

Her father was a native of Meerut in north India who had settled in Assam. There, he started off as an English teacher at a higher secondary government school in a block called Kalchini and later became its principal. Her mother was Assamese. She would go about the household chores humming and singing folk songs. That's where Ratri first picked up music. Her sister Chitra was six years older to her. Shyamal, her brother, was four years younger. She had not seen him for seven years now. And the last she had heard from him over the phone was three years ago. He had gone to Venezuela in search of work as an engineer and settled down there after marrying a native girl.

Chitra arrived annually from Gujarat where her husband worked in a power plant. She would meet Ratri and then go on to Assam to stay with their parents, who were lonely, and disillusioned, waiting for their only son to come and spend time with them – a flying visit at the least, typical NRI style. In much the same way as their neighbours' children arrived from across the seas, flashing goodies, distributing a Casio watch here, a tie there, ten-dollar perfume for the ladies, a few chocolates to the kids and a hefty cheque or maybe just a video player to Ma and Pa. They would never stay more than a week in a small place like Kalchini where a mere cable TV channel could not be received properly.

Ratri had not known life beyond Kalchini till she was nineteen, although she had been to Guwahati a few times with her Bihu troupe from school. But never on her own, all alone. So, to her it had meant a great voyage to travel to Delhi with her troupe, which had been selected to represent Assam at the Indian folk dance festival. Delhi was turning cosmopolitan in those years. There, in the audience, she had met a quiet student of medicine from Delhi, Tarun, who had come with a bunch of zealous classmates much too eager to lay themselves like Persian carpets at the feet of the girls and waltz away to love or a harmless fling, whichever clicked. Tarun devoutly attended all three days of the festival, and by the time it ended, he mustered up enough courage to ask Ratri for her postal address and phone number.

He proved to be far more romantic than Ratri had anticipated. He had a reticent but passionate side to him and Ratri was in a daze till six months later, when they were married in a small ceremony in Kalchini. Immediately after finishing his MBBS, he took the first train to Assam and brought Ratri as his bride to his ancestral home in Delhi.

She was still standing at the window. Nayan thawed the silence: 'Ma, can I wear the gold bangles Papa gave you on your wedding? They are lovely. I want to wear them to Jeeban's marriage. I know you're possessive about them. But can I wear them just once?'

Ratri was humming.

Tohri baat takat hare naina...

Nayan repeated her plea. 'Ma, where are your bangles which Pa...'

'Hmm?' Ratri asked, sounding remote.

'I sold them.' She turned and went to the guest room to do her evening riyaz with Guruji Maharaj while Rani posted herself near the door as usual, the everyday audience.

Nayan listened, stunned, through the evening.

Saajan woh din kaun thay,
jo sukh se laage nain
takat haare nain ...

(Beloved, what sorts of days were they
when I fell in love with happiness,
I lose myself searching for them now...)

The longing expressed in the thumri gradually smoothed out the crease that the wedding bangles had etched on the habitual placidity of the household.

One, two, two 'n' a half!

Jeeban is playing Ghalib on his archaic but charming inheritance of a gramophone that his dead grandfather left behind for him. Salil sits, eyes closed, a tiny notepad in his right hand and a pen in the left. Meera is making a slow, calculated move at chess. She moves the horse, 'one, two, two 'n' a half' – *ek-do-adhai*, like her father had taught her – she almost says it aloud.

Jeeban hums along with the record. He is watching Meera. How different she is from the others! In her off-white silk sari with turquoise blue elephant motifs on it, she looks lovely. Looking at the gold band on her ring finger, he feels lucky to have her in his life. How happy he is with Meera, how content. Touch wood! I am being such a softie, eyeing my own joys. And touching wood, like a woman. But it's true that falling in love makes you stronger and vulnerable at the same time – wise and silly, deep and frivolous, horribly nervous and utterly confident. It brings

you closer to your compassionate self. Maybe that's why you get in touch with the feminine in you, the more sensitive side of you. Love brings you closer to your inner self, it takes you to your core, but the damn thing also pushes you to the edge! It's intoxication, it's sanity. It's the best and worst of everything. It's a different life, a life that teaches you to surrender, to accept, to become a part of someone else's universe…

He speaks up on a sudden gush of excitement, 'So how about some Scotch on the rocks? It's a beautiful, leisurely evening. Does anybody want anything? Meera? Nayan?' Nayan is standing and watching closely the hundreds of potted cacti lined up on the terrace parapet, the floor, and hanging from rusty iron hooks on the terrace roof.

Meera says, 'Yes, I'd like some chai on the rocks please!'

'Chai on the rocks? What on earth is that?' Jeeban laughs.

Nayan joins in: 'Well, you could say, ice tea.'

'Ha! You people are uncultivated when it comes to matters of taste. Missing out on one of the best things in life,' quips Jeeban.

Salil wakes up from his reverie when Jeeban hands him a glass of whisky.

Meera says, 'Come on. It's your turn now, Jeeban. Let's see whether I let you win this time.'

'Oh, not to worry, madam-ji. I have already lost myself to you a long time back!'

They all laugh at Jeeban's theatrical admission.

Humming along with the record, Nayan comes back to sit with the three.

Qafas mein mujhse rudaad-e-chaman kehte na dar humdum
Giri hai jispe kal bijli woh mera aashiyaan kyun ho

(Don't hesitate in relating news from the gardens inside my cages, my beloved.
Why should I make that nest my home, which was struck by lightning yesterday?)

Suddenly Jeeban says, 'Hey Nayan, why don't you sing? I mean, why don't you try becoming a professional singer? You could sing Ghalib. In fact, you could even try some of our younger poets to begin with. There are so many people writing now.'

He pauses a while. 'Okay, I know what to do to give it that initial push. A get-together at my place any evening, with all our friends, acquaintances, press colleagues and seniors to play audience. Mirza Asadullah Khan Ghalib and Scotch on the rocks! How is that?'

Letters

Salil wrote to her too, mostly ordinary little notes from the places he travelled to. She aired them, knew them word for word, phrase by phrase, with all the pauses and full stops.

Sonapani, Kathgodam

It's chilly here. I am uncomfortable sleeping in a tent at this time of the year. But, one can't deny that there's an unmatched fun to it, raw and uncut. Was fed up of the studio, so got here without telling you. I am getting you pines for a gift. And, sincerely hope that I shall post this note to you tonight.

God bless till I see you next. And much more after that.

Salil

Valley of Flowers

Uphill, in the valley of flowers. A picture-perfect place to be in, to live as if in Illyria of *Twelfth Night*, dream-like. Just flowers, innumerable flowers everywhere, as if a rainbow has burst into a million shades over this expanse. Which raga will you be singing today with your mother for riyaz? Sing Jaunpuri and I shall hear you say '*Phulwan ki gendan na maaro…*' God bless you.

Love,
Salil

Gangotri

Did not know where to go. So I came away to see the glacier melt and flow. Have been thinking about you. Dreamt of you in that off-white brocade sari you wore to Jeeban's wedding. Your mother's gold jewellery looked good on you. You should wear saris more often, you know. Pehna karo sariyan kabhi kabhar, achhi lagti ho! I can see the glacier from this rock here. I have named it after you.

See you here and hereafter. Will you come?

S.

Haridwar

I have come here after almost fifteen years. My last trip to Haridwar was with Mum, Dad and Sameera. Sameera was thirteen then, prancing about at Har ki Pauri in a polka-dotted frock. I still have that image of her in my memory. She wore matching ballerina shoes to go with her dress and her hair was in two pigtails, a silly hairdo I never liked.

Is this the first time I'm telling you about them – Mum, Dad and Sameera, my little sister? Haridwar reminds me of lotus leaves laden with marigold and burning diyas that my mother and Sameera floated on the Ganga at the time of the evening aarti. I remember being amused by the upsurge of chants in unison from crowds completely disparate in appearance, languages, even culture. I remember touching Mum to check whether she too had goosebumps all over like I had. Sameera sat on her haunches on the pauri, lapping water downstream to set sail lamps being floated by others. She has been married for three years now and lives in Bradford with her husband and his family, which moved from Pakistan to England to start a garment business there. She met him in Cardiff where she went to do a course in finance. Our Sameera is Zahida now, converted before her nikah with Firoz, the only son of an otherwise unorthodox Muslim family. She gave up her religion for love. She offers namaaz five times a day now. Whenever I hear the azaan at the mosque near my studio, I imagine Sameera on her knees, her forehead covered with a bright silk veil, murmuring verses from the Koran. Almost at once, I see little Sameera from another time, setting afloat marigold and earthen lamps on the Ganga in Haridwar.

Dehradun

Dear Nayan,

Have come to spend some time with Mum and Dad. I will be here a couple of weeks now. Will get you stick-jaw candies from here. You will love them. Dad is very busy with his flower seed sale, orchard and stuff. We played rummy last night, over rum and kebabs. Ma makes delicious reshmi kebabs. So my time here is going all hunky-dory, rummy-rum, rummy-rum, rummy-rum.

Sameera is still a sore point, stumbled upon every night at dinner. They miss her very much.

S.

Saharanpur

My dear N,

I have been smoking incessantly with Raghu at whose place I've been staying for the last few days. We had twelve packs yesterday, and we've smoked them all. Bad boys! Tch, tch, tch…

Raghu's a bright guy. He and I, we were together in school, all twelve years. He runs the biggest bookshop in town. It's called The Read-INN. He sells music too. Apart from that, he's mostly preoccupied with a small school his aunt runs for special children. He makes amazing chicken on the barbecue almost every night in the small lawn outside his cottage, while I lie on a hammock under the open sky, playing on my mouth organ. It's Don McLean's turn tonight, *'Starry starry nights, paint your palette blue and grey...'*

It's cold here. A fizzy cloud comes out when I exhale.

> ...look out on a summer's day
> With eyes that know the darkness
> in my soul...

Hey! I am getting pangs of separation now... Stay well. I'll be back soon.

Salil

My heart feels like a dark void, a black hole

Again the breeze of morning wafts its fragrant bloom
Breaking its cage, the bird that is the soul, flies to Him
AMIR KHUSRAU

She spends her days in the guest room, oblivious of everything. She runs her fingers over the patterns embroidered on Guruji Maharaj's kurtas that still hang in the wardrobe. She takes out his gold kurta buttons and dangles them in sunlight to see the inlaid emeralds glint. She sits on the floor, staring blankly at the empty bed. Both their tanpuras lie quiet, untouched. In the evenings, she sits for hours on her straw mat. Ragas don't come to her these days. Rani calls out to her several times, coaxing for orders, and sobs in private, getting no response from her mistress.

Tarun has slipped back into her life, giving her silent company. He has stalled work to be with her. His gaze follows

her around like a shadow in the house. There are no words between them now, no rebukes, nor complaints. Not even an exchange of silences.

Ratri had gone quiet over the last ten years or more, while he forgot to notice how she had kept the house and their lives going. She swept up all her sounds then and took them to the riyaz room to nourish them differently, to teach them to search out an alternate identity. Slowly, she had almost gone invisible. As if she had covered herself with a pall and decided to live subliminally. Her impression was visible everywhere though. Even so, something had changed. She was present in the house all right, but as if behind the curtains, or in the pristine white lace of the crochet tablecloths. She would move soundlessly around the house doing her chores. She never forgot to change the flowers in the vase every morning. She would organize Tarun's clothes as usual, give them out for ironing, put the ironed ones back on hangers, give the used ones for washing, but without pausing to smell them for a whiff of him like she would earlier. She would still brew his tea, just the way he liked it – light, black, with tulsi leaves and no sugar. But she would send the tea upstairs through Rani. It was not anger. Ratri was not a resentful person.

Maybe it was him. His aloofness, his self-absorption had injured her spirit. And now, with the recent loss, she looks disturbingly still, as if trapped in the quagmire of her sorrows, like a dead fish. Pictures turn like slides in the kaleidoscope of her mind, the tanpura chords weaving them all into one continuum. Guruji Maharaj singing Bhairavi at dawn.

An awestruck twenty-year-old girl touching his feet. Raga Madhuvanti echoing on many afternoons through the years which had brought her music, womanhood and motherhood. Guruji Maharaj singing at Neel's naamkaran ceremony. Lying on the bed in the guest room, telling her about his life, teaching young Nayan while narrating stories from the scriptures. His last days in her house. And his last journey that began from there. Images flit and cross her mind and come back again and again until she remembers by heart which picture follows which one.

One morning of no Bhairavi. One afternoon with tranquillity as his song, he lies in unadulterated peace in the sitting room. His ganda-baandh disciples sit around, adorning him with flowers. Ratri sits at his feet, applying sandalwood paste to them. Deep inside, she feels like an old hag of a spirit one moment, a disciple of twenty in another. The long stretch of time between her initiation – her first lesson – and her last surges and ebbs turgidly, like a dying sea, in her memory.

On the thirteenth day after his death, a group of disciples sing sitting before a big photograph of him performing in Vrindavan. Nayan sits holding Ratri's hands. Ratri is floating in and out of a mesh of memories. A Hari bhajan ends and a young disciple of fifteen picks up the tanpura after bowing before his photo. She hums a little and begins to sing.

'Na kou tara, kou na raat
Udi jaihein re jaaye waara
Paache chaiyde kou na raag

Na chanda, na raiyn chidayyiyan
Udi jaihein re jaaye waara
Ankhiyan mori neer ujaas’

(Neither a star, nor the night
The departed soul flies away
Leaving only silences behind
Neither the moon, nor a night-bird
The passer-by walks away
Leaving behind tears in my eyes)

Her voice soars through the thick mist of incense. It touches the roof and sprouts into echoes that melt the silence that plagues Ratri. Weeping buds of pent-up sorrow break into wild, black blossoms within her. Countless, endless whorls – whole fields of them. Brittle and dark, the colour of hopelessness. Tears flood her eyes. In a broken voice, she says turning to Tarun who is sitting beside her, ‘He had said he didn’t have a child. I was the daughter he never had.’

The black flowers, thousands and thousands of them, crumble to ashes.

Possession

A month later, Veeren, a young lawyer disciple of Guruji Maharaj, came to meet Ratri. He entered the sitting room where Tarun and Ratri sat reading. Handing over a small parcel to Ratri, he said, 'Didi, Guruji's bank papers were handled by my father. He asked me to get these back, using whatever money was left in his accounts, before he passed away.'

Ratri opened the packet and took out a pair of heavy jadaau bangles.

Curious, Tarun questioned her after Veeren left. 'What did you do with those bangles? What were they doing with Veeren?'

'Sold off some of my jewellery and mortgaged these for Guruji Maharaj's treatment. I didn't want to disturb you in your research work to ask for help. You did not, but I guess, Guruji Maharaj noticed they were missing from my hands.'

Away, on his butterfly wings

Salil calls up at three in the night from Saharanpur, high. On weed perhaps. He doesn't talk, just keeps singing and laughing. The song he croons is also playing in the background. It's a recent number.

'Dil phuko aur itna phuko
Dard pighal jaaye
Zindagi sulgao yaaron
Gham nikal jaaye'

(Smoke your heart away
Till all the pain melts
Light up your life, friends,
Let all the sorrows go)

It's after five months that he has called. One fine day, he

shut his studio in his usual nonchalant manner and left without letting Nayan know.

She has been waiting for him to call or show up since. But they never had any promises to keep, or conditions to abide by.

'Time is not my cup of tea, re baba. And place? One fixed address? I have never had any since I left school.'

The question had implicitly risen and sunk many a time. 'Where will I keep you, and till when?'

Sometimes he would say, 'Maybe we could wander together forever. But life goes awry the moment I sketch a plan for it,' he had said time and again.

They were together unconditionally and if they were to part, it had to be unconditionally so.

He had written on the walls of his studio once:

'Kabhi toh saal-saal parvaan charhe
Kabhi ishq apna sifar hai ek lamha'

(Love may prosper for years on end sometimes
And just one moment may turn it into a cipher
sometimes)

Cold creeps in through forgotten louvres

Untimely rains had driven the weather wild. There was heavy snowfall in Himachal and Kashmir. All over Delhi, people were pulling out broken furniture from their attics to burn them; the electric heaters and blowers had given up. Rani had stuffed newspapers in the louvres of the windows to keep at bay the fierce winds that blew after midnight when the clouds let up. Newspapers every morning mentioned ten or twelve people who had died of cold on the footpaths.

Nayan was just back from a concert by her mother. An unpleasant evening. Someone's mobile rang twice just as she had begun. Ratri was on the alap. She stood on the bank of a river, its transparent water lapping at her feet. She had to descend into the raga, walk down the steps of the ghat and take a dip in the river. Guruji Maharaj would say the keys to the 'mahal' or castle of a bandish hung on one of the surs in the higher octave of the glass corridor that an alap was.

One just had to look carefully. 'Your voice has hands and feet that can sculpt the raga. Touch the walls of the alap lovingly, but with caution. There are some notes that are *bahurupiyas*, impersonators from neighbouring countries who may look like the one you're searching for. If you touch them, a trap door may open under your feet and you will slide into another country, another raga!'

Like Guruji Maharaj, she dwelled over the alap for long, ascended from the mandra saptak to madhya saptak, from madhya to taar saptak. To Nayan it was like a bride entering the door to a new house. Opening one door, entering another saptak or octave, looking around to see, and then walking forth with all the grace she could muster, to open another door, and then door after door. On opening the gate to taar saptak, one met the high notes – taar Sa, Re, Ga, Ma, Pa... Now that all the three worlds were open for her, and she had reached the gates of Guruji Maharaj's 'castle', she could sing with abandon, frolic as if she were playing with water that could flow freely across the three octaves. Ratri had almost lost herself to Raga Madhuvanti and found the key to the 'mahal' when the cursed mobile rang and kept ringing till the ustadji on the tabla yelled through the mic and asked the proud mobile owner, whoever it was, to leave the hall. Ratri, having been recalled from the high gates to the 'mahal', did not react. She just stopped singing for a while till the accompanists called the manager and had him ask the audience to switch off any more phones that were still on. But the silence within had been stirred, the rhythm of the harmony violated.

Nayan felt drained. She slipped into her room quietly and lay flat on her bed, stretching her hand to dim the cane lamp that hung from the ceiling close to her bed. The night was darkening. A very deep blue was quietly creeping into the layers of air and age that lived in the house.

She could hear her mother talking to Chitra in the other room. Chitra Masi had come down to see them and her own parents in Assam. She could hear them chat like sisters often do, Ratri no longer a silent, lost listener of a monologue, as it had been since Guruji Maharaj's death.

Late into the night, while they sat close to the fireplace, Chitra sang lovely Assamese folk songs and told stories of their childhood – Ratri's, Shyamal's and hers – to Nayan. Nayan had named her the migratory guest. She flew in every winter like a migratory bird, chirping happily and humming songs from the past. Nayan was almost tempted to call her CC Masi. Chirpy Chitra.

These days her father had consciously begun to trace his feet back home. Was he too like a migratory guest? Who knew. The phone rang. It was Jeeban.

'Hello Nayana Devi! Where have you been? You alive? Or, have you forgotten us?'

'I'm fine, Jeeban. Just a little tied up with Ma's concerts. You tell me, how's life? How's Meera doing?'

'She is well. Busy. Another exhibition up her sleeve. Portraits this time. You are coming to the inauguration. It's on the twenty-eighth of this month.'

'Waah, that's great. I shall surely be there.'

'Have you started singing yet? Our plans of hosting your launch party have been delayed, not forgotten.'

'No, Jeeban. Ma will take some time. I know she thinks I'm not ready yet, and I agree with her. She's been very tied up with her programmes. I need a thorough six months' riyaz with Ma, if not more, before I can even think of going solo. Ma did not sing at all for many months after Guruji left. But then his students organized shows and urged her to perform again.'

'Any news of Salil, Nayan? Where is the wanderer? Is he in touch?'

'Nah…he doesn't feel the need to.'

'Nayan, do you want me to come over? Do you feel like talking? I'll come and take you out for coffee, if you feel like it.'

'Maybe some other day, Jeeban. I'll see you guys on the twenty-eighth.'

That night, Nayan dreamt of old banyan trees growing out of her room walls, filling it with long, twisted branches and long, snaky roots that came hanging down from them. She was walking on water inside her room; it did not seem to have a floor any more. It was like a dark, bottomless well. She began to sink. She frantically tried catching one of the banyan roots so she could climb up back into her room and out of the dream. But she kept sinking deeper. The abyss of night echoed with the ripples of water. Then, she somehow caught a root and heaved herself up the well with great difficulty. She climbed up a branch and sat there. There she found a little girl seated on a facing branch. She looked exactly as Nayan did in her childhood. Legs dangling from the branch, she sat reading Salil's poems. And as she read on, Nayan saw her gradually grow up into herself. Suddenly, it began to rain. The ink on the papers in the girl's hand was washed away, and she started turning into an old woman. Wrinkles crept up all over her sagging face, the eyes sank into their sockets, and grey hair emerged from nowhere. That, Nayan saw, was her face.

She woke up, her breath caught, beads of sweat on her forehead. Could love lead to psychological ruin of this kind, Nayan thought. Yet she could manage to look perfectly normal when she walked out of her shell, her room, which amounted to leading a double life. No one knew, though Jeeban had some idea, of how she suffered for Salil, for the irretrievable loss of each day lived without him. Life was passing her by. She wasn't really part of it.

Opening the wooden casket, she sat up to read Salil's letters under the cane lamp. Its filigreed light swayed in the slight wind that had found a passage through the slats in a window Rani had missed blocking with newspaper. It threw little patterns of pale light and shadows on the letters. Nayan was scared of stillness. The play of light in the wind calmed her somewhat, assured her of change.

She began to read. All of them – the letters, the little notes and poems. And yet, she read them insanely, repeatedly. Her eyes searched frenetically for a new shade of meaning each time, a renewed sign of validation.

Memories of their meetings fluttered in the room like restless butterflies. They rustled in her mind like dead leaves riding the wings of an autumn breeze. They kept humming in her nerves like a mighty swarm of bees. She knew they would haunt and chase and tease her for many, many light years. She felt tired. Her soul was festering.

Neel

Nayan's brother Neel has been away from home for five years now. He had left soon after finishing college, with a documentary film-maker friend of their father's. Neel had found Palash Mitra formidably interesting. When in town, Palash would drop in every Friday for a drink or two with Neel's father. Tarun was very fond of him. They had known each other since school. Neel would miss the last few lectures and come back early from college to join Palash and his father. In those days, Palash would talk at great length about his forthcoming series, which was to be based on the tantric cult in India. Neel would listen to him intently, secretly admiring the adventurous life Palash had.

After Neel finished his bachelor's degree, he expressed a desire to get into film-making, to join Palash on his project. Tarun, like any other parent, wanted him to study further, but Neel put his foot down, pleading with Tarun and assuring him that he would enrol himself in a long-distance programme and

get higher degrees if necessary. Ratri tried telling him that he could pursue whatever he liked but after a few years, by which time he would know better which way to go. Neel had left at twenty-one while Tarun was travelling out of town on work to join Palash who was shooting then in the Kamakhya temple, eight kilometres west of Guwahati.

The day Neel arrived in Guwahati, Palash stood at the location, clad in a rugged pair of jeans. His shirt hung loose over a slight paunch, a much-used, dull silver Parker and a tiny notepad sat in its pocket. A brown, black and white chequered cap covered his fast-balding pate. His photochromatic glasses could only half hide his eccentric eyes because they were loose and kept slipping down the bridge of his long nose. A grizzled beard and a thick greying moustache drooping down to a pointy chin completed the picture of this man who was a caricaturist's delight.

Neel followed Palash down a flight of steps into the Kamakhya cave. There lay the famous Kamakhya, not an idol of the goddess but her reproductive organ, the 'yoni'. Neel wondered whether the devotees who came here remembered at the time of praying that what they were pouring milk and gangajal over, covering with leaves and flowers and khoya sweets were actually the genitals of God. These were a people who considered any talk of sex blasphemous; their children came as if from immaculate conception. In this very culture did they pray to lingas and yonis of gods and goddesses. Neel found this contrariety rather amusing.

'According to the legend, Kamakhya came into existence

when Sati gave up her body after her father King Daksha insulted her. This enraged Lord Shiva. He started on a Tandava of fury, cutting his wife's body to pieces so that no one would cremate her. Sati's 'yoni' fell to the ground at this spot where the temple now stands,' Palash explained.

People from his team prostrated themselves before the 'yoni' and prayed in silence for a few minutes. Neel stood behind them, wondering in amazement what brought thousands and thousands of pilgrims to this place where he was standing with his mentor-to-be. He had often heard his mother mention Kamakhya. But somehow he could not bring himself to relate to the religious enthusiasm he saw in the others. A person's religion, he thought, had to evolve through life experiences; it didn't matter which religion one was born into.

'Neel, we will begin shooting in the hills first,' Palash said. He looked like an archaeologist, Neel thought. It then struck him that Palash resembled the character Marco in R.K. Narayan's novel, *The Guide*.

'So Neelratan, let us proceed with the planning of shots now. Let's go back to the hotel and do the storyboard?' Palash said. Neel had just got an extended, new and rather unattractive name.

Yes, Marco! He spoke in his mind, attempting to avenge his re-christening. 'Yes, sir,' he said, loud and clear. He thought of what it would be like if Palash ever married and had a wife like Rozy. Would Neel have played the naughty guide then? Wow! His life would be mighty interesting in such an emotionally and sexually charged situation. He sniggered as he trudged behind Marco Polo.

Neel admired Palash's faith in his work. He took mental notes of everything he thought was relevant and began assisting him with absolute sincerity. After a few months, in a place called Tarapeeth, near Deoghar in south Bihar, Palash told Neel one night over dinner, 'You have inherited that aloof gene your father has. Tarun's seriousness has got into you, too. Keep it up, Neelratan! I think, I need not worry about who'll succeed me.'

Neel was tall like his father. He wasn't very strongly built but had a lanky, athletic frame. He had Ratri's eyes, sometimes aloof, sometimes intent; they saw through everything as though the world was a big glass house, and the people and places in it were all made of glass. He had a quiet disposition, a sharp, subtle wit, a very restrained body language, and long artistic hands like his mother again, the nails of which had begun to turn yellowish from incessant smoking.

He would spend the whole day wandering places with Palash. At night, he would write his travel diary before going to bed. Ratri would often receive postcards from Neel. He sometimes wrote to Nayan too, rare letters about lessons learnt on his journeys.

Dearest sis, Nayan,

Trust you're fine. I'm doing good. Writing to you after several months, so you deserve a long letter this time.

I have met countless new people on the road in the last few years. People from different states, different cultures, diverse strata. There is one thing common to all the people from the generations before us. An overall sense of contentment and happiness with their lot – with the kind of lives they have led, with the set route of their lives, marked by milestones of customs, rites and rituals, and engagements like religion, domesticity and society to keep them busy. Naturally their lives have been much simpler than ours. They haven't had strange questions confronting them doggedly all the time. Questions that seem unanswerable. They havent felt uncomfortable in their own skin the way we do.

Our generation is the warped lot, Nayan. A strange inadequacy plagues us. We have everything, but we still want something more. And we mostly can't put a finger on what it is that we want. Even young people in villages now – let alone the youth living in cities – breed ambitions that might surprise you. The desires of people like us sometimes get fulfilled even before they take seed in our minds, because we happen to belong to our families. Nevertheless we remain hopelessly deficient, restless, and saddened by some unknown, impalpable grief. We run after elusive dreams, creating illusions, and mourn violently when the bubbles burst. What are we looking for? What is it that will satiate our thirsty souls? I have been thinking about this very often these days.

Palash Uncle is fine. We have been struggling with

the Saraikela administration for a permit to shoot the sacrificial rites during Durga puja that are about to begin in a couple of days. Saraikela is a very small place, a six-hour drive from Jamshedpur in the south of former Bihar, now Jharkhand. From an empty field here, I can see the border of Orissa, too. You must ask Ma. She would know about Chhau dance. There are several Chhau training schools here. These dancers use beautiful masks made from papier-mâché. The white masks are stunning for their starkness. I will parcel you one from here. This place was a monarchy before Independence. A palace still exists in the middle of the town. It's now in a shambles, though. I met the last king's youngest son just yesterday at a teastall. He had pulled up there on his rickety Atlas cycle. He would have succeeded him as the king now, had monarchy not been abolished. I had a long chat with him. He said he would help us shoot the Ashtami puja performed in the Pauri Devi temple inside the palace premises. Later I gathered from the local residents and hangers-on that many, many years ago humans were sacrificed to appease Pauri Devi during Dussehra. Commoners are still not allowed inside the palace and the shrine. Only descendants of the royal family can watch the rituals.

We have been put up in the government rest house here. Soot-black cobwebs hang low from the ceiling almost over my head. Power comes and goes as it pleases, at super-quick intervals. And mosquitoes are playing a biting symphony around the mosquito net under which I sit writing to you. You can imagine how much I must miss you to be writing at this hour, taking such pains under such conditions. But all this has a wry charm of its own – the cobwebs, the crawling spiders, roaches and rats running riot on the floor in the dark, and hyper-green frogs jumping around in the loo.

Have bought peacock feathers for you from the local mela. They also do a lot of papier-mâché work here. Shall send Ma a pair of papier-mâché pigeons soon.

Let's see what happens at the SDO's office tomorrow morning. He is a young, dynamic man from Bihar, very sharp, and serious about his work, I've heard. However, his subordinates are very high-handed and standoffish. That's counting in the many sarkari peons who hang around doing nothing much except feeling unreasonably possessive about the wooden stools they sit on. They don't want us to meet the SDO for some reason and keep deferring our appointment with him. God knows why.

It is an interesting place; a small, removed, microcosmic world in itself. So, I really don't mind staying on a little more. I hope Ma and Papa are fine and you are taking proper care of yourself. Really miss hearing Ma and you sing.

Loads of love,

Neel

The second coming

Salil returned one morning after a whole year. Rani led him to the guest room where Nayan sat with her mother, singing Bhairavi. Ratri sang and Nayan followed her notes. Salil stood quietly at the door, listening. Their voices seemed to be coming from the core of a conch shell. They resonated, tapping the walls of their consciousness, searching perhaps for a shared epiphany. He knew he would take these voices with him on his journeys. They would come back to him and echo like sweet memory in the hollow caves of his days where he would hide away from the ratty world, writing his ghazals.

Nayan with her eyes closed looked... complete? Quiet? Ethereal? No, he did not have the right word at hand in that moment. Her hair fell loose down her back as always. Wavy, brownish-black curls now shone red, now gold in the early morning sun.

She looked mature. Salil realized she looked older than

the last time he had seen her. Her fingers were constantly strumming the tanpura strings. The youthful restlessness of her fingers was gone. He remembered going to Gandharv Mahavidyalaya, where she performed once in a while with her friends, to hear her sing. She would play distractedly for a while and stop in between while singing; perhaps she was too conscious of her surroundings then. Now, she looked complete, and serene, singing after her mother. Her hobby was turning into her vocation.

Suddenly, he felt an urge to leave. He would have slipped away had Rani not appeared with a cup of tea.

Salil had never met Rani. In fact, this was the first time he had come to Nayan's house. He got a little flustered and stood where he was, tightening his hold on the freshly bound book he had brought with him.

After leaving Delhi, Salil had not really made an effort to keep in touch with her, except sending some letters but those had also been erratic. He had missed her though. Missed her voice, her disjointed, meaningless and meaningful chatter, the sudden aloof silences in between sentences, and the rare but uncontrollable laughter after which she would suddenly start humming a song, closing into herself, shutting the doors of her private universe, that invisible city inside her which no one had a key to. She was his secret raga. She had played in his thoughts on his aimless journeys. She had chased after him like an apparition in his poetry. Lingered in the air around him, like the scent of a woman whose perfume stays on in your room long after she has left. He had often mistaken other girls in new places for Nayan. They had all seemed like her at first glance, but totally alien the next moment. There were very few like her. Maybe none.

Nayan meant so many things to him. She meant a world of songs, one for each mood, for every season. She meant reading together from a pocketbook edition of *Divan-e-Ghalib*. She meant pink-skied and burnished evenings when she sang some of those ghazals for him. She meant moments when he thought all his moorings had dissolved, for meeting her had freed him in more ways than one. Yet, she was the only one who could make him return to herself again and again.

He had been with other women before. They had brought him pleasure and trouble and all kinds of other things, and he had moved away from their worlds, not wanting to drop anchor. The thought of going back to see them always tired him. They were all women of the world, demanding and forever gushing. Nayan, he thought, was like the secret preserver of mindmaps; she understood or could make allowances for any kind of irrationality. She was like a gatekeeper to his generation's undecipherable melancholia. He liked her small, inexplicable sorrows and her fetishes for little things like the perfect bookmark, a certain tree on a certain street in central Delhi, or a box of first flush tea that her grandfather sent her from Assam every birthday.

Making love to her was like reading in a new language, in a new script each time. It annoyed him sometimes that she asked him innumerable questions in bed; that she wanted to know about all the places he had travelled to, down to every single detail, that she planned imaginary trips with him to the hills, forests, rivers, the seaside just when they were in the thick of things. As their bodies moved in a newfound sync, they mapped new territories of love and want.

He adored that her hair got caught in his watch each time and there ensued a little struggle in the dark to extricate it from his 'time' as she referred to it. Why couldn't he just throw the damn watch away? It had stopped years ago and he hadn't had it fixed, but he wore it every single day, all the time, except in the shower.

They read for hours from a new book each time after they made love. They both read obsessively; their bodies were made of books, Nayan said to him in jest sometimes. She would move on to other ideas soon. She would like very much for their bodies to be made of laughter. Feverish but sparkling, sharp-edged laughter. That body of books or laughter, when he entered, gave his hands the power to turn her skin around in his hands as if she were clay. She could be a new woman, a different body each time.

Their little obsessions and inadequacies had brought them together. They could walk through life, holding hands, strolling across innumerable seasons in time. But an irrepressible urge to flee from a settled nest, an aching discontent with familiarity caused him to escape every time. He needed grief in his life to live it, to move on. He needed emptiness and disorder around him, so that he could go on living, wading through time, travelling away from those who knew him to those who did not.

Rani came up then, dragging a cane chair and softly whispered, 'Bhaiya, sit down and listen. How long will you stand?' Salil sat near the door, making sure the two singers would not see him if they happened to open their eyes.

Ratri led her on, lining the notes, adorning the imaginary form of Bhairavi, the dark goddess, with jewels from her voice. At some point, the goddess emerged in flesh and blood and held her hand. Ratri began walking with the goddess, tracing back her feet in time, to her youth in Guwahati, to Kamakhya, to Kalchini, to her school. In her mind's eye, she saw herself with many other girls her age, dancing the Bihu. They all went in a half circle, then back, and then a full circle. Very slowly, as if in a trance, dancing to songs that could not be heard.

Then Nayan tripped on a note, as if she were uncertain, not knowing whether there lay a ground beneath her feet. She coughed, trying to clear her throat, groping for the right notes. A deep inner emptiness surged upwards from her navel and gurgled in her throat. Several shades of one note emerged in a tangle and jostled each other. Then came a sequence of notes. She tried to catch the end of that string of surs. It was trailing like the tail of a torn kite in the agitated hollow within her. She felt as though her voice was stretching its hands to grab the string, but it kept slipping away. She tried humming in a parched voice but choked again.

Like she had choked when she had tried smoking...? She had lit up one of the stubs from her father's ashtray, she had told Salil once. She had always been curious about cigarettes.

Then she had choked again at Qutab complex, while she sat with Salil near the second minar; that unfinished Alai Minar.

Nayan finally regained her ground, retrieving her voice from the cobwebs of her mind perhaps. She was singing smoothly now, the rishabh, the gandhar, dhaivat and nishad flowing in sweet camaraderie. The songs of Bhairavi were parting from their voices like flowers and wafting in the house like perfume. They were singing in unison now – mother and daughter. Two souls in communion. The Guru and the disciple.

A book reopened in Nepal

A letter bearing a Nepalese stamp arrived. It was in Neel's microscopic hand. And it looked like there were many letters this time, not just one. His letters were like mementos from different places, whiffs of various spices and stories. This time it was from Kathmandu.

8 November 2003

My dear, dear Nayan,

Hope this finds you in good health. I have an intriguing story to tell you.

We were in the middle of a very interesting assignment, trying to recover some of the earliest soundless videotapes shot in India in the royal estate of Darbhanga (a district town, four hours from Patna), when Palash Uncle suddenly decided to chuck it and leave for Nepal.

A fortnight ago he told me one night that we needed to stop work and go to Nepal, just him and I. The rest of our team could go back to their homes for a holiday. His tone conveyed he did not mean to explain why.

So, the next day we hired a taxi from Darbhanga to Birganj on the Indo-Nepal border. An eight-hour drive got us to Birganj from where we caught a cab to Kathmandu a day later. Palash Uncle told me we were headed for his maternal grandmother's home. Though his grandma was long since dead, his mother's youngest brother still lived there with his children.

They were surprised to see us; his uncle and family. Palash Uncle had not informed them of his visit. His maternal uncle, Chhoto Maamu, proved to be an interesting character. Over seventy years of age, he retired as the manager of the Assam Tea Company. He had extremely sharp eyes, an angular face which must have been handsome decades ago, and longish braided hair. He moved around wearing a maroonish silk robe tied in place with a long orange ribbon throughout the day.

I spent the next two hours there drinking China tea from a mug deep as a well, and devoured a plate full of arrowroot biscuits. I discovered Chhoto Maamu has a huge collection of matchboxes, 2263 different brands from all over the world to be precise, pasted neatly in a red velvet-covered scrapbook. And, what's hilarious is that he religiously plays Ludo with his grandchildren Choku and Debi every day.

Chhoto Maamu's wife passed away three years ago. He has three sons. Two of them work in the Assam Tea Company while their wives and children live here. The youngest, Rangan, is studying medicine here in Kathmandu.

Our first night in Kathmandu passed in celebration of Palash Uncle's arrival. Chhoto Maamu is quite a loquacious character, ever ready with wisecracks and clever jibes. He must easily be the most foul-mouthed man I have met; he coins the filthiest and most unusual cuss words at the drop of a hat. His eyes, Nayan, his eyes betrayed somehow that he knew why Marco had all of a sudden undertaken this journey to Nepal. And that too, after thirty-three years.

Okay, I'm about to doze off any moment, so let me stop this letter here. Will be back soon. Give my love to Ma and Papa.

Yours,
Neel

9 November 2003

My lovely sis,

Hope you're doing good. Suddenly remembered it's Jugnu's birthday today. She would have turned twenty-eight. I sometimes wonder if we'll ever recover from the shock of her suicide.

Anyway, I was telling you in my last letter about how we reached Kathmandu. Marco wasn't there when I woke up the next morning. I was told he had gone out after downing his first cup of tea. Chhoto Maamu ordered Rangan to take me sightseeing. I agreed readily.

When Palash Uncle did not turn up for dinner, I went up to ask Chhoto Maamu whether he knew of Marco's whereabouts. He was engrossed in a game of Ludo with Choku and Debi. 'Chhoto Maamu,' I asked, 'any clue where Uncle might be found?'

He shuffled the dice in his closed fist and threw it on the game board.

'Two!' said Debi, animatedly. 'Dadu! You only move two houses up the board.'

'Two houses away from ours,' Chhoto Maamu said, looking at the board still.

Shuffling the dice again, he threw it once more on the board.

'Six!' Choku cheered.

'Over five times six years back in time.' Chhoto Maamu smiled at me and looked out of the main door beyond the entrance, towards the road which led to the temple.

'No cheating, Dadu. Only one turn is allowed. Remember the rules?' Debi cackled, snatching the dice away.

'Son, life is like this game of Ludo,' he told me. 'Man shuffles the dice, takes his chances and moves forward in time. But he keeps coming back to the bends in the road which have shaped or scarred him, even after those bends have crumbled to ruins and all that's left of the past is a site the awaits excavation. He comes back when what he thought he had forgotten rises from its ashes. Like the city of Pompeii in Rome… The heart is one such city, son. It preserves memories in its dark alleys. Here one can't afford a long forgetting…' Chhoto Maamu laughed. He leaned back in his chair and looked at the false wooden ceiling, talking to no one in particular. 'Memories are made of something invincible. And they regenerate before you can even wink!' He was nodding his head from side to side as he spoke. 'One moment they are like motes of dust. Then, before you know, they coalesce to form a face you can instantly recognize. They may be flung away. Far beyond the seven seas of time if you please. But they never forget their way back. Like the salmon that return, travelling for over two to three years sometimes, from the oceans to the rivers that they were born in, bruising themselves, half-destroying themselves on the way.'

'Dadu, why don't you play seriously?' Debi cribbed.

'Oh! But I thought I was the only serious, non-minor Ludo-player left on this planet. Neelratan, you see, everyone plays the game oblivious to the truth of playing it throughout their lives.'

'Rangan!' he called out. 'Go and see whether Palash is at the temple.'

'Chhoto Maamu, I'll go and see if he's there,' I suggested.

'Okay, child. But do not get lost like him. Otherwise I'll have to send another person after you. Walk straight across. It's not far away.'

At nine in the night, I set out to look for Marco in the direction of the temple. After walking on uneven, sloping roads for about fifteen minutes, I entered a chain of alleys. The narrow lanes, lit up with a zillion little round bulbs, were lined with bright little kiosks selling heaps of shivalingas, big and small, made of marble and granite and mother of pearl, rosaries of wood, pearls and coral, and mounds and mounds of vermillion. Inching my way through those crowded lanes, I reached the Pashupatinath. Entering the two-storeyed pagoda first, I saw a giant shivalinga. I looked around for Marco in the crowd which was beginning to dwindle and disperse, but I couldn't see him anywhere. Huge bells tolling inside the shrine began to ring in my ears. I came back to the front yard of the temple and panned my gaze beyond the huge Nandi bull in the centre and the cluster of rather phoney-looking sadhus telling their rosaries near it. Nowhere could I see him. I then walked from the southern side of the pagoda behind the parking area towards a stony bridge. I could see a row of fires burning, some blazing and some already turned meek. The air above was doused with smoke. As I walked closer, I saw more fires along the length of the riverbank. They were funeral pyres, lined up like two banks. Between those banks of the pyres, below the bridge on which I stood, stretched the black river, Bagmati, turgid and lazy like a long sleepy serpent, having swallowed the ashes of the countless dead. I was filled with a strange mix of revulsion and fear.

Upstream were caves and shacks of Shaivite sadhus who come to Pashupati on pilgrimage. The river, its ashen gloom, and the awe-inspiring crackling gold of the pyres on its banks – the sight made me dizzy. Just then, I saw his silhouette. He stood still like a wax model on the far end of another stony bridge upstream. Walking across the bank, on to that bridge, I called out to Palash Uncle. He seemed taken aback to find me there.

'You came looking for me, did you?' And then he said, 'Let's go back. It's time.'

Achha, will write more later about this very soon. Have to go out for a bit. You take care.

So long,
Neel

10 November 2003

Hey sis,

Time to kill. So let me get on with what I was telling you yesterday. Where was I? Haan, yes, at the bridge. So, Marco and I walked back home without talking that night. In the next couple of days, we hardly saw much of Palash Uncle at home. He would disappear early morning and come back late in the night very, very preoccupied. Both the daughters-in-law of Chhoto Maamu would keep muttering about Marco while cooking. I would find him engrossed in himself, on the banks of Bagmati, behind the temple, every night. I had no clue as to what this sudden change in his behaviour could be attributed to. He seemed pretty much off his hinges. And I kept wondering why we were still in Kathmandu, and how a workaholic like Palash Uncle had not mentioned work even once.

One morning I woke up to find Uncle writing at the desk. I felt relieved to find him there. Seeing me get up from the bed, he said, 'Neelratan, you can pack your bags now. We shall leave tomorrow morning.' As he walked out of the room, I dared to blurt out, 'Uncle, can I accompany you today?'

'Where?' he asked sternly.

'Wherever you go. The temple maybe?' I said.

His forehead furrowing, he nodded a 'yes'.

That morning we walked to the temple, past the cluster of sadhus and tourists. Some of them were busy smoking marijuana in preparation for the full moon that night. The others were chanting mantras. A medley of drones suffused the air around. One man's mantra blurred into another man's murmurs. I thought it would be impossible to sort out the mantras from the air, they had almost stitched themselves on to it.

Clearing our way through the jamboree of devotees and goats and cows and dogs, we reached the side of the temple that overlooked the black river. Palash Uncle walked with sure steps towards a woman, rather girl, who sat in a corner reading a tattered book. She must have been around nineteen or twenty years old and had a chiselled but wan face; a neat nose, thin lips, big but insipid, expressionless eyes. On seeing us, she stood up. I noticed her hair, a thick black braided shiny rope that reached down to her knees. Rapunzel in Nepal! I thought. Uncle greeted her with a warm but restrained smile. The girl returned it with a slight curl of her lips. Then her face set again and assumed a somewhat stern look. Uncle introduced me to her saying, 'This is my friend's son and my talented assistant, Neelratan. Neel, this is Gehna.'

I could feel an awkward silence fall between the three of us. It was a breezy day. The wind loosened a lock of Miss Rapunzel's hair. She tried carelessly to tuck it behind her ear. One could see slow ripples in the Bagmati. The flames of burning corpses were running astray after the breeze. I tried to look for an appropriate line, a topic to kick-start a conversation with Marco and Rapunzel. But all I could think of, looking at the river, was death. Nevertheless, I blurted, 'It looks ghastly. Doesn't it?' turning towards them. Gehna spoke this time, in a tone as cold as her big eyes. 'No, not always. It means love to some people. It has meant so…'

I wasn't prepared to combat such profundity. I did not quite understand her purport. Moreover, the void that replaced the need for small talk now suggested I'd better shut up and look on dumbly.

I stood wondering where this Gehna girl had materialized from. I had never heard Marco mention any such girl in the past. Funny thoughts swam through my mind. Maybe Uncle had now decided to make feature films, and this Miss Gehna was his debutante heroine-to-be.

I could see a couple of urchins struggling to fly kites in the distance across the river. The kites would rise and fall limp again and again. Very much like the lack of connect between the three of us. Words would launch out of the silence like kites and then fall flat to the ground. The three of us must have stood there like three points in a line for nearly twenty minutes, gazing at the pyres burning away to cinders, leaving clouds of dark smoke behind.

Having begun to feel restless, I decided to walk around inside the temple complex. I realized that I was an intruder she might not have liked to speak in front of. I had guessed right. For I found them talking when I came back half an hour later. The book that had been in her hand when we met was now in Uncle's. Seeing me approach, Uncle suggested we have lunch together, and very unexpectedly we had Miss Gehna accompany us to a restaurant a little further away from the temple. There I came to know that Gehna intended to move back to Calcutta where her father lived and where she had lived till a month ago, to pursue a course in fine arts at Santiniketan. But that is all I learned about her. After lunch we walked back home, leaving her where she lived, two houses away from Chhoto Maamu's.

We spent some time with Chhoto Maamu over tea, devouring a trayful of arrowroot biscuits again. I sat discussing Nepal politics with him till Choku and Debi dragged me away to play snakes and ladders. I heard Palash Uncle and Chhoto Maamu discuss Gehna in hushed voices. Their voices became less and less audible, and I could barely hear a thing by the time I beat the two kids at the game.

All right, looks like I need to pause here. The rest shall follow soon. Marco's sent for me. We're all going to Pokhara today – Chhoto Maamu, his daughters-in-law, the kids, Rangan and us. A little picnic there. Will get back soon.

Love,
Neel

12 November 2003

Hi, little sister!

I am back.

Have stolen away from the living room. Though Chhoto Maamu wasn't quite ready to grant me this reprieve from his censure of the ruling Shah dynasty of Nepal. I need to finish telling you this story tonight.

That night after dinner, Marco sat reading through the book Gehna gave him. It was a book of Tagore's poems. An hour later, I saw him step out of the house,

stories about pigeons – how they lived in the rafters of the roof; how they spoke to each other; how they held their parties, festivals, weddings and funerals. Often she would sit surrounded by children, relating gruesome tales that made one's hair stand on end. Swapping fictitious characters with real names from the neighbourhood, she wove such gothic incidents around them, they would send a chill up my spine. She was always buzzing like a bee around the house, whizzing past like a spirit, anywhere and everywhere, her awesome tresses trailing behind. But they said, the women in that household – Deeda and all my aunts – that women with beautiful hair never lived beautiful lives. They always rebuked her for leaving her hair untied, flying in the air. They used to say, some day a bad spirit would get caught in her hair and make its house there.

'I stayed in Kathmandu for three months, for more reasons than one. The most important of them was Mishti. She was infectious and irresistibly distracting. She was intelligent, perceptive and had a vivid imagination. She demanded every little detail about Calcutta from me, and scoffed demeaningly at my description of it, swearing she would never go to a city which had old ancestral houses crammed together in such a way that if you put a hand out of your window, it would stick inside the neighbour's. She swore she would never step into my city.

'Mishti and I often went out with a bunch of kids from the house, she leading the gang of course, to Pashupatinath and this river. Gradually we took to coming here alone, on our own, she not leading any more, but walking by my side. We walked till the Bagmati every evening. She told me of every myth she knew about Nepal. Occasionally, she launched into bouts of singing. Her voice was heavy and hoarse and she sang so badly that I had to put a ban even on her humming. How immensely out of tune she was! I loved nagging her about it. And so Neelratan, the responsibility of singing fell upon me as if it were a necessity – singing in love. Not that I was a great singer in any way.' Uncle laughed.

'Yes, we fell in love. We realized it first. Then Deeda, and then everybody in Deeda's household. And later, Mishti's parents. But that happened much later. In fact, after I left for the States. My three-month-long love story suffered a rude jolt when my admission letter arrived from America and I had to pack up and leave. I left Maithili, promising to return and get married to her. I left for Calcutta, leaving my copy of Tagore's poetry with her. She cherished the book as long as she lived, always writing to me through those years I spent in America, saying, she loved Tagore but hated Calcutta; courtesy, my description of it.

'A year after I left, her parents came to know of our little story. Deeda tried to explain that we could get married when I came back after two years. Two years on, I got a scholarship to another prestigious and specialized course, and also a chance to make my first documentary series. I had to stay on for two more years to make my films and work there to pay off the loans I had taken for them.' Uncle paused, then continued. 'The last letter from Maithili said she was getting married to someone from Calcutta. Her parents couldn't wait any longer. They did not wait. My work finished after a year of her marriage to Anirban, a distant relative of my father's maternal aunt. Everyone gets connected to everyone somehow in the end.

'Maithili, who loved Tagore and hated Calcutta, was sent to a joint family in one of Baghbazar's well-known ancestral houses to live with her husband who taught history at the university. Maithili, who loved Tagore, made my only gift to her, her secret-keeper, her diary, her catharsis. She hated each day of her life in Calcutta away from the Bagmati here.

'I met her once in a pujo pandal, nearly a year and a half after her wedding. The pandal was packed with hundreds of men and women and children. It was chaotic, the kind of chaos that could bring two people together or tear them apart. A chaos of delight, a chaos of desire, a chaos that could break us into pieces. My chatty Mishti looked quiet and pale. She was heavily pregnant at the time and looked extremely sick. That was how I last saw her – a spark stirred in her eyes and went numb.

'I travelled without a pause after that – doing projects, assisting senior film-makers, making short public welfare ads. I worked like a machine. Some of those films were so tacky that I threw them away later, tearing up the tapes inch by every inch. I went on working madly, mindlessly, all those years... Almost three decades have gone by.

'Two weeks ago, I received a letter from Chhoto Maamu. It was written over a month ago, but it reached me late since we keep moving all the time and my only permanent address they know is my mother's house in Calcutta. So, the letter got redirected from there. It said Maithili had fallen very sick with some sort of incurable intestinal disease. There were perforations in her gut. She died after living her last days in Kathmandu. Her only child was staying with her parents for some time before Anirban came to fetch her. Gehna is Maithili's daughter, Neelratan.'

The singer

Nayan had sung with her mother in concerts a few times, accompanied her, filled the gaps in between her alaps and taans like any shishya would do. But her first solo public performance as a singer was at Jeeban's house, on his and Meera's second wedding anniversary before Jeeban's friends and colleagues from work. She started out a little nervously. There were just too many people looking at her with a patience that looked somewhat precarious – there one moment, and poof!, gone the next – and a little too obliging. But, she gradually settled as the evening went by. An hour of pure classical – vilambit khayal, chhota khayal and tarana in Shankara – and then another hour of ghazals as requested by the guests. Jeeban and Meera sat at the back of the room like proud parents, assuring her with their warm smiles that it was going all right. Before she could conclude the soiree, the thought of Salil slipped in like an autumn leaf, through some window in her

mind that she had forgotten to latch. And as she sat sewing one note onto another, he knocked... No, why would he knock? He never sought permission! Just barged in. No, not him. Just the thought of him.

And then, she said she would sing a new poet – Salil's ghazal set to music by her.

'Khud se bekhabar ik lamha
Sham tak dopehar ik lamha

Kaise tafseel se bayaan ho firaq
Ke mera naambar hai ik lamha

"Kaash" ke naam kitni hasratein udhaar raheen
Purshish-e-naambar hai ik lamha'

(Oblivious of itself to age forgets one moment,
Till evening an afternoon stays one moment

How does one narrate the details of separation
For I am granted for narration one moment

'If only' owes me countless unfulfilled desires,
Your messenger to hear me out spares but one moment)

After she finished, she stood up and her listeners got up, too, to congratulate her. They asked her questions and showered her with compliments, all at the same time: Have you been learning music? How long have you been training? Who do you take lessons from? What a nice voice! Do you sing at weddings? It's my daughter's wedding next month. Will you come? Can we not have another session with her, Jeeban? You are quite young to sing this way. You rock, yaar! You will go places. So when do we get to hear you next?

Nayan's mind was whirling. She tried catching each question to answer it and kept saying thank you's in between. But something was slipping like sand through her fingers. She wanted to lock her fist tightly around it. What was it? She felt tired of the questions. Sanity. She was losing it. And she was conscious of it. It all seemed so nebulous – the people around, even her own voice giving muddled answers to clear questions. It was disconcerting, this free fall into a conscious delirium. She was caught in another spate of appreciation when one question struck her hard, splintered her nerves and pulled her back to the moment:

'Who's this poet you sang last?'

She got a grip back on herself as if taming the storm inside her head, as though gathering all the dry leaves that some savage shift in the earth had thrown up in the air like a tornado and, tying them up with silence calling it a day.

Soon she got a chance to sing at a music festival sponsored by the group that owned Jeeban's newspaper, *The New Delhi Times*. But one year on, Nayan took up a job with the same newspaper to report on art and culture.

In the newsroom

She strained her ears to listen, but couldn't hear anything except for a babble. It seemed to exude from the crowd in the office cafeteria. No, she could not hear what they were saying, however much she tried. Her colleagues Srilata, Tina, Jennifer and Hari were discussing something. The latest Bollywood release at PVR perhaps. And she was supposedly part of this conversation, a passive one though. This wasn't the first time she was struggling to hear people sitting in front of her, talking to her. The other day, she had sat next to a famous Pakistani singer. The moment she asked her first question, snap went her link. She could not hear what the singer was saying in answer to her question. Was it a disease? She had no clue.

'Do you think we can go for *Tumhari Amrita* tomorrow after work?' Srilata inquired, slurping the curry from her plate. 'Can you finish work early, say by five, so that we can catch the six-thirty show?'

So it was a play and not a film. Yes, she remembered. It was a famous one, with Farooque Sheikh and Shabana Azmi in it. It was being restaged in several cities across the country. The story, she recalled, was about the exchange of letters between ex-lovers. Letters… She had also written some le-tt-ers!

'Haan, I think I'll make it by four thirty-ish,' Nayan answered. 'Do you think I can get Ma along if I leave office at that time? She used to be very fond of Farooque Sheikh's films.'

'Yeah, sure. I'll arrange for six passes right away.'

New Delhi Times was a colossal organization and Nayan felt like a tiny speck in that universe of people who came rushing in by the minute with reports from all corners of the city, and then rushed out again, hunting for more news. It was a crazy place, the office, especially after nine in the night, when the pages had to be fitted and readied for press, when ashtrays filled to overflowing with cigarette stubs and the newsroom transformed into a smoggy box that almost choked her, with nails being chewed in desperation, and pens and pencils and sheets and phones flung about in panic. But strangely, this madness brought her sanity. It kept her going. The daily flashes, however brief, from the lives of colleagues who negotiated antsy Delhi days typing away at the keyboard for hours on end lent her a chord on which to tune her own time. The reporters who made grand entries into the office talking animatedly about diverse events of the day – a press conference, a Hindu-Muslim riot, a servant murdering an old couple for money, a Congress leader visiting his constituency in a helicopter and eating dinner at a dalit's hut, an actor's wedding, a cricketer's stormy affairs, a footballer's zillion children out of wedlock – filled her days with wonder. Countries, people, love and war, all converged at an unbelievable proximity and floated about, turning into scraps of newsprint. Then they changed avatars, became sandwiches, muesili and parathas the next morning that could be chomped on by millions at breakfast. This space by itself made for a very readable potpourri. People snitching on each other to bosses to gain brownie points, people having flings with more than one colleague at a time, workaholics who did not go home for days, alcoholics who carried liquor to office in waterbottles, and shopaholics who blew up every paisa of their salaries in the first week of the month on retail therapy. Then there were the cribbers and the jabberers, the backstabbers and the shirkers, the faffers and the jokers.

Nayan was observant, no matter how lost she looked. She was staring hard even without looking in your direction. She liked knowing that she could vaguely imagine what went on in other people's homes and in their minds. She was a fast worker and did not mind covering inane events because they gave her a chance to see and meet all kinds of people, real and fake.

One person in office who intrigued her very much was crime reporter Hari. In his late twenties, preposterously chauvinistic, utterly confident about his looks, his dress sense and language skills, occasionally throwing some gallant, outlandish phrases at you to prove his point. Everyone on the staff agreed that he had an uncanny understanding of the criminal mind, and that he could easily reconstruct the events that might have led to any particular crime that hit the city papers before the cops or the CBI could, just by analysing the prima facie evidence and statements from the parties affected. Others on the crime beat, Bhasker, James and Patil, secretly envied his confidence and ganged up against him time and again, claiming more credit than they deserved, making a big show of their stories.

Hari was overbearing, talkative to the point of being irritating, pompous too when it came to showing off his work. But he meant no harm to anybody and his concern for his friends and colleagues sort of redeemed him. However, there were certain things no one knew about him. Nobody knew where Hari lived. Nobody knew which way he went after leaving office late at night. He generally came in around noon, worked till two or three in the night, and disappeared after that as swiftly as a cat.

Nayan had once asked him.

'Russia!' pat came his reply. And then laughing out aloud, he had said, 'Purani Dilli, silly. Where else? I have told you so many times.'

They had struck up a friendship founded on a simple equation: Curiosity was good so long as it came from him. Hari was interested in Indian classical music, so Nayan and he never ran short of things to discuss when sitting in the office cafeteria. He also faffed a lot on topics that made for great conversations anywhere. He said that he was from Karnataka but his parents lived in Egypt, and that he had two brothers, two sisters and six dogs. But no one could tell for sure whether this was true. That definite air of mystery surrounding him, Nayan thought, made him interesting to talk to. Most people at *New Delhi Times* were curious about him. He moved very quietly, on the tips of his toes almost. No one with their back to the door could hear him walk in until he spoke, or placed his hand on their shoulder.

It was a rainy day in July. Hari walked into office quietly, his usual verve missing. No loud Hi-s! nor How-goes-the-day-folks. Nayan looked up from her cubicle. She noticed that he looked visibly upset. He did not talk the whole afternoon, just kept sitting quietly.

In the evening, Nayan walked over to his seat.

'Hi! What's up, Mr Holmes? Come, let's go down for chai…?'

He got up and followed her to the cafeteria and sat on a chair with a thud. Slowly, he sipped tea in unsullied silence. Nayan sat wondering what the matter was with him.

'Do you think we can go out for a nice cup of coffee tonight after I finish? Come, I'll treat you today, Hari,' Nayan ventured.

Hari answered, 'No… some other day Nayan…' His voice was quivering, like a dry leaf in the breeze.

'Don't you think you'll feel better if we go out…?'

'Umm, okay. We'll leave at nine,' Hari acquiesced, almost stuttering and not meeting her eye.

At nine, after they finished filing in their stories for the day, Nayan and Hari set out to the nearest coffee shop in Connaught Place. Nayan looked up and down the list of assorted coffee on the menu card.

'What will you drink, Hari?'

'Anything… just about anything will do, Nayan…'

'Would you like to try Irish coffee? They make very

good Irish coffee here,' Nayan said, trying to make Hari feel comfortable.

'Yes... that will do.'

Nayan placed the order and paid the bill. Collecting the receipt, she looked at the other side of it. She remembered how Salil scribbled poetry on them while Nayan would sip her coffee. She would say, 'Those slips are mine...' Salil would counter, 'They are mine. I will throw them away into the bin on our way out. It's just to fill time while we talk.' She would insist on paying all the tea coffee bills in order to keep those slips. She still had so many of them lying in her bag.

'You know what Hari, I always drink Irish coffee here because it reminds me of a friend who...'

'...is dead?' Hari stuttered even before she finished.

'Yes... But how did you know?... And how do you know such things?'

Hari didn't answer. He was looking outside the window at the cars on the road.

'What is the matter, Hari? You've never been like this before. What is disturbing you so? You can tell me.'

His voice as impassive as the expression on his face, Hari said, 'It's this case I have been following since late last week. A girl committed suicide or was murdered...pushed from the sixth floor of a building in Janakpuri. Nothing has been established yet. No clear proof nor eyewitnesses.'

'Yes, I read that story,' Nayan said. 'What about it?'

'The girl did not live in the apartment building. The people from the building said they did not know her. It was only yesterday that the police found a pair of sunglasses on the staircase that connects the fifth floor to the sixth floor. Since the building has a lift, nobody thought of using the stairs or even checking it once all these days. The police also recovered a letter and a snap of the guy the girl was dating. Her neighbours had seen them together. Today, the police brought him from Jaipur for interrogation.'

He looked at the table top and into the mug.

'Why is it disturbing *you* so much? I mean, you deal with such things every day. What is it, Hari?' Nayan asked again.

'He killed his girlfriend...' After a long pause, he added, 'Exactly the way my younger sister was killed three years ago in Bombay. She was nineteen then, dating an MLA's son of all people. The fool believed he was in love with her. My parents had warned her, but she did not listen. He cried at her funeral. But I saw it in his eyes. The police said she fell from the terrace of a five-star hotel. They said she was partying and was very drunk. The case was closed and we had to leave the city forever.'

Hari's voice broke. His stiff mask of self-confidence melted away and tears rolled down his face.

The bride from Nepal

Nayan came home to find Neel's letter lying in the mailbox. He had met Gehna again. Palash Uncle was staying in his Calcutta home to take care of his bedridden mother. Neel was generally loafing around, doing nothing much, so Palash Uncle had sent him to Santiniketan to meet Gehna.

> 'I've been meeting Gehna after college hours for the past three days. She is a nice girl; very different from what she appeared to be on our first meeting in Nepal. She mostly talks about her mother. After I come back to my lodging, I read Maithili's diary. It is lying with me these days, though Gehna doesn't know about it yet. Some of her entries are deeply moving. I am copying down and sending you some pages from her diary. It isn't right but I want you to see them, because you will understand.'

Maithili's diary

5 April 1972

I sit under the tap in the bath, with my palms joined edge to edge, open and spread like a lotus. Water falls with great force from the tap and a torrent of bubbles jumps on my palms and scatters. It's my second week in Calcutta, in my husband Anirban's home. The house is a clutter of dark stairways and passages running up and down, around the rooms, to the terrace, and the courtyard below where my mother-in-law sits with her mother-in-law discussing what is to be cooked today with the wives of Anirban's brothers. It is in one of those passages which leads to Panna's room that I saw a shadow-like thing the other day. It was a woman for sure. The room has remained shut for years now, says Anirban. I went to check it one afternoon when no one was around. The women of the house were savouring their rice-induced post-lunch siesta locked in their dank yellow box-like rooms. I could only see a dusty bed, a table, a rickety chair and an almirah in there. The almirah was in a state of complete disarray. It contained some bordered *taangail* saris, a few books and a little carton full of glass bangles. Anirban said that she loved bangles. Last night he showed me a photo of her, his youngest unmarried sister, Panna, when I asked what she looked like.

It's strange that nobody in the house mentions her ever. Anirban says she died of typhoid some seven years ago. But the other day, his eldest brother's fifteen-year-old son, Tukai, told me Panna had consumed rat poison, but his mother told him that she had gone mad. And all this was to be kept secret. Yes, I'm sure it's her I saw. It was her spirit walking across the passage that goes to her room.

It's been an hour now. Soon they'll come looking for me. This dingy bathroom is a haven away from the family. I get to think inside here. I sit in a corner and read Rabindranath or write on the margins of this book. In between, I play with water from the tap. It reminds me of home.

The torrent of bubbles is still falling on my hands. It almost looks like the water's oozing out of my skin. It's the Bagmati – the witness to my love, my life – that has come bursting out, ripping apart my nerves, and scattering away, flooding, submerging my immediate reality... this house that I live in as the new bride from Nepal.

20 May 1972

Tukai's bought a bright red kite from the bazaar. He insists that I go up to the terrace to fly the kite with him. I tell him that I am writing something and will join him upstairs in a few minutes. But the impatient boy goes down to the big courtyard and complains to my mother-in-law that the new kakima is writing something and not helping him play. Pat adds the maid that she's also seen the new boudi scribble away something in a *khaata*.

I am called downstairs and told, 'Andhokar ghore boshe kobita lekha ei poribaar-er-jonne kokhonno shubho hoyni...' (Writing poetry in dark rooms has never proved auspicious for this family). I go upstairs without answering and fly the red kite with Tukai thinking why I am being told this. I don't write poetry. I don't know how to. This is just my quiet monologue. A secret one.

17 June 1972

The frogs are croaking hoarsely. Rainwater drips down the roof onto the house walls. It has been pouring the last two days. The clouds looked like they were crying, beating their chest against the rotting wooden windows of my room. Come June, this place gets flooded by rainwater, first flowing like a river and then stagnating like the stubborn memory of a day spent in love. I stand in the balcony of my room and open my palms. Water trickles down slowly from the roof to my palms. I tilt them and the water falls two floors down to the road into a big pool of water.. A college-going couple crosses the street, wading through knee-deep water. The girl lifts her sari to her knees. The boy's upturned trousers get wet at the folds. They hold a book between them instead of holding hands, and walk through that lake of grime, bliss written in large letters on their faces. As they turn the bend in the road, I can see only their backs; it begins to rain inside me. I feel like weeping, howling out aloud, and calling to them: 'Wait. Turn back just once. Look in my direction, please. I wish to see the monsoon, its joy, its love and longing, suffuse your faces.

25 July 1972

Anirban is home, playing bridge with his brothers in the big hall downstairs. I can hear them discuss the latest in Bengal politics and the President's rule that ended a few months ago, and crack a joke or two in between. Their laughter cackles through the house. All the four daughters-in-law stand in the background and revel in their collective happiness. I walk across the verandah, turn left at the end and climb a short flight of stairs to Panna's room. Slowly unlatching it, I slip inside. I throw the window open first. It's difficult to breathe with so many years of dust covering everything inside. With the loose end of my sari, I begin cleaning up her things: the desk first, then the chair, the almirah and then the dusty bed. I take out the books from her almirah – *Sonar Tori*, *Raktakarabi*, *Nashtoneer*... so many books – and blow the dust off them. The first page of each book bears her name in a faint blue, curvy hand.

Poornima Chakrabarti
46, Baghbazar,
Calcutta.

I open a mildewed copy of *Dak Ghar.*

> 'I can see [...] the King's postman coming down the hillside alone, a lantern in his left hand and on his back a bag of letters climbing down for ever so long, for days and nights, and where at the foot of the mountain the waterfall becomes a stream he takes to the footpath on the bank and walks on through the rye; then comes the sugarcane field and he disappears into the narrow lane cutting through the tall stems of sugarcanes; then he reaches the open meadow where the cricket chirps and where there is not a single man to be seen, only the snipe wagging their tails and poking at the mud with their bills. I can feel him coming nearer and nearer and my heart becomes glad...'
>
> in *The Post Office, Dak Ghar*

It has begun to rain again. Soon water will come pouring in through the window. Closing the windows, I latch the door, quietly come back to my room, and change into a fresh sari.

1 August 1972

Anirban is a nice person. Uncomplicated and calm. He never asks me what I write in this book all the time. He never asks me how many more times I will read it, nor how many times I have read it so far. He lets me be, and says we need to become good companions for life. And

I say, I'm trying my best. He talks very little. Only when spoken to. His elder brothers talk a lot. I hear them talk from seven in the evening when they get back from work till ten in the night when they go to bed. Anirban sings well. He sings Rabindra sangeet, never loudly, but very softly, sitting up in the bed before going to sleep sometimes, looking at the ceiling, his hands crossed behind his head, or in the evenings as he stands in the balcony, thinking something or nothing in particular. I feel like asking him to go on till the sun rises again.

15 August 1972

I am telling Tukai a ghost story. He stops me in the middle of the tale to say he has seen Panna Pishi in the house many times. Is it her ghost?

5 November 1972

Two days ago, I was caught sitting in Panna's room by the maid. I got a warning from the family not to overstep my boundaries again. I was just sitting there reading one of her books. The room looked habitable again after a clean-up and a fresh bedspread on the bed. Anirban was furious for the first time since we were married. He flew into a rage when his mother told him about it. He kept yelling at me for almost half an hour, but I could not make out anything he said in the hustle of the buses, taxis and trams shuttling on the road outside. I could only see the changing colours on his contorted face.

8 January 1973

It's a cloudy day. I chop vegetables sitting in the courtyard in the midst of the womenfolk. The jingling of their bangles fills the lull that lies between the sound of their breathing. Twelve rohu fish lie ten steps away from me. Dead, with eyes open in a blank stare, ready to be dressed, sliced into pieces, fried and dropped into a shorshe-batar jhol for lunch. Anirban's mother sits on her armchair, crocheting a money pouch and looking up in between, towards the upper floor of the house, with a sense of pride and reassurance. The maid comes and begins scaling the fish one by one, telling the elder boudis of her domestic travails. I wonder how I have managed to survive almost a year in this household, away from Nepal where I was born and brought up. Suddenly, I push the knife away and hurry up the stairs to the balcony of my room. I look down and see the same couple passing by, holding a book between them, their faces turned away from me yet again. I feel hysterically withdrawn – writhing in remembrance. Nauseated. So much that I wish to vomit, scrape every bit of it and spew my soul out. I weep wretchedly for an hour or more on my bed, wetting the desolate white bedsheet.

24 March 1973

Everyone is fussing over me. They say I'm expecting. I am going to be a mother. I feel miserable and remain shut in my room, feeling nauseated all the time. Yesterday I thought I saw Panna sitting beside me on my bed. I was scared, but she just sat for some time and then disappeared like a dream.

4 October 1973

I somehow pick myself up to attend the Pujo with the family. We go around in a mini bus hired specially for the purpose of pandal hopping. How else can such a big family go together? The Fiat we have is too small for all of us. We go around the city all day from one pandal to another, zigzagging through Calcutta's insufferable traffic. The weather is nice, the smell of dhunucchi from the aarti and shiuli flowers trailing us everywhere we go. We bow down before Ma Durga's indescribable grandeur. Everything around her is festive and aglow. People are celebrating her return home; she has come to her mother's house for nine days and will return on bijoya dashmi to her husband's place.

It's evening by the time we reach Maddox Square. Boys and girls dance with dhunucchis in their hands. I'm tired. I can barely stand on my feet any more. I feel heavy as it is, and the bunch of silver keys tied to the end of my sari and flung over my back weighs me down. I begin to feel nauseated again and wait for the family to finish so we can go back. It is then that I see Palash. Ma Durga is playing games with me – this puny puppet in the toy world that she created to amuse herself. But he is for real. He is there, face to face with me. 'Kaimon aachho, Mishti?' he asks when my elder sister-in-law summons me. 'Boudi, come, come! We are boarding the bus!' I want them to stay on just a bit longer. Just a few more minutes, for god's sake, please. No, for an eternity probably. I have to answer how I am. I have to tell him. But I just stand there like someone made of wood, not knowing why time always runs out when he is around. Anirban comes then to take me away. And I walk away with him, towards the bus, then I am inside it, crawling through the Calcutta traffic again, back to my room, my ivory tower in Baghbazar where I live. Why is the goddess playing with me?

'Well, it's a small world,' Anirban says when I tell him about the man in Maddox Square whom I met at a neighbour's house some years ago back home in Kathmandu. But I know, I know that this world will swell up and turn so vast that I will never see him again. That man in Maddox Square, and I will get lost in this big wide world, and not meet ever.

1 November 1973

Away from Calcutta, where the daily circus of marital life slyly pushes me towards insanity, inch by quiet inch.

Here in Kathmandu, back home, it's raining memories as I walk towards the Bagmati. My child quivers inside me, growing and turning in my womb, making a mother out of me with every passing breath.

Bagmati, I did not forget you for a moment. You who pull my infidel shadows towards yourself with such urgency. Bagmati – this endless vein of darkness flowing through my soul which is cut open, lacerated by memories of those months that I still preserve... This river of death that flows past Nepal, this sanctum of Shiva where I came to know Palash was the one I loved.

15 November 1973

My daughter is in my hands today. Six days old. A little birdie from some other world, her hands and feet so unbelievably small and tender. I'm scared to touch her, lest my worldly roughness should hurt my delicate bundle of hope.

They have sent for me to return to Calcutta. Just the thought of going back from Kathmandu pains me. But this time, I have a reason to live. That I could shelter a life, that my baby was formed within and drew strength for nine months from the well of tears inside me has restored my belief in life. I have a reason to live – to see her grow each day. My child. My jewel. Gehna.

Poetry is a pack of lies

Concluding the riyaz, Ratri bowed before Guruji Maharaj's garlanded photograph in the room, and touched the tanpura with her forehead, joining both her hands. Nayan did the same and, laying the tanpura to rest, came out of the room. Salil stood up, a half-smile on his face. Nayan looked at him. It wasn't disbelief but an uncertain elation with which she asked, 'Why, how come you are here?' Where have you been all these months? she wanted to ask, but her hurt pride held her back.

Ratri came out of the room straightening the end of her sari over her shoulder. On seeing Salil she said, 'Nayan, ask your guest to sit.'

Tying her hair into a knot, Nayan led him out to the lawn under a canopy of lemon trees. He sat down on one of the cane chairs placed there, hiding a little book he was holding. 'It's pleasant here in this tiny grove these days,' she said and

looked the other way. Then turning towards him, she asked, 'Why have you come? You think you can come in and go out of my life as you please? For one and a half years you don't care to inform me of your whereabouts. You write letters that are not dated. There's no address for me to write back to. What am I expected to infer from that? What is it with you, Salil?'

'I came to give you this.' Salil handed the book to her.

She took the book.

A Pack-o'-lies, said the letters embossed in gold on a plain red-clothed, hardbound cover.

She turned to page one without looking up. It said,

'First things first. I need to return all my incomplete jottings to somebody. I have finished them, though I know my muse will say they remain incomplete. What more can one do, sometimes words just don't suffice.'

My verses
Are like burnt-out stubs of time,
They are hours that turn to ashes
When love smokes me out,
'n' I travel like a charred spectre
Black in the face,
With soot in my nails
From your universe
To my homeland,
Scribbling, scratching, scrawling

Etching with nervous fingers
On my mind forever, a pack of lies!

Nayan looked up at him and they both laughed. So much that Rani came out of the kitchen to peer at them, surprised.

Between the middle and the edge
Hanging 'n' not hanging from the ledge
Of love, I fall every time in thought
You are profound and I
A shallow, doping, vagabond lot.
And yet,
Between this slip and your thought
On this edge or that ledge
Come light years
In split seconds
Of searing desire
That you sweep up
From our game of coffee,
To make memories
For the voyeurs of romance to
Make pink albums with

They laughed together at the title, the dedication and his first publication. That evening they met Jeeban and Meera to give them a copy of the book.

Salil read out to his three-member audience on the terrace of Jeeban's house. Meera poured out tea for all of them while

Jeeban sat listening, his right hand on his chin. Nayan watered the cacti pots one by one.

Wasn't it for love
That I met you
On a road one afternoon?
I hated you for usurping
My idol away from me
Hated you for that extra rupee
I paid for your cup of tea
Detested that unspoken right you
Had over that book
I had so desperately wanted
Ached irritably for walking down with
You for the sake of my master
And for the hundred little sacrifices
I made all the while
Not smoking nor showing my miff
But there was something I liked,
Rather loved, I would say,
Our shadows walking together
Ahead of us, merging,
Then separating,
Criss-crossing ways
In the playful sun,
And, that subliminal shadow
Of a quiet, calm confusion
That crossed your eyes

As I said I'm done,
Before you left that day

'So, Mr Poet, you met your muse on the road and fought with her over a book?' Jeeban teased.

'All lies, as the title suggests!' Salil said and laughed, sipping his tea.

Removing a dead leaf from one of the cacti, Nayan looked up at the sky. The setting sun was hiding behind clouds.

'Seems it'll rain tonight,' Jeeban said.

'Oh, bless you if it does. It's become really sultry,' Meera replied.

That night it rained in sheets after midnight. Thunder and lightning startled the listless summer skies. Nayan stood near the glass door in the passage outside her room. She wrote with her fingers on the wet and misty glass.

I wish to fall on my knees
And cry miserably today,
Your tears, not mine.
Come, let us swap
The dark clouds in our souls,
And laugh so much out of joy
That tears well up in our eyes,
Mine in yours and
Yours in mine,
Like the blue rain of remembrance
Like the pearls of two lives intertwined

Let us live each other's lives,
Your dawns, your sun and shadows
If not one,
Seeking to know
If not all of you
In the least,
A drop by little drop

She laughed, looking at the trees outside. They were swaying wildly, like crazy witches. She saw something moving on the steps at the door outside and bent over to see what it was. Bozo stood sticking his muzzle against the glass, all wet and splattering the water off his body. Nayan opened the door and pulled him in. She dried him with a hair drier, then put him under her bed and switched the lights off.

Then rose the tender sun
One morning
She and I
Uncertain
But happy
She pulled the curtains apart
And gold champagne
Came pouring into our lives
And flooded all the lanes
I walked through the day…

She went and woke Salil the next morning. He was staying in

a friend's apartment. He got ready and they started walking towards the bus stop.

'Where are we going?' he asked.

'ITO, to the *New Delhi Times* office,' Nayan said.

'Oh good, Samar, Firoz and Manto will be hanging out near Mandi House. I can meet them and get updates on what our Marxists are up to these days... But why *New Delhi Times*? Do you need to meet Jeeban?'

'I have been working there for the past three months. And it's a working day today.'

'Oh, I didn't know. Well, good, you have come really far. Jeeban told me that you sang at a few places in Delhi these last couple of months and you are going to Gwalior next month with some other artists.'

Nayan remained quiet. She had come to tell him of her new job, her first public concert. But something had stopped her. She realized she did not wish to update him.

'Well, wish you all the luck in life,' Salil said, his face betraying no expression.

Clearly, he was hurt. But there was nothing she could do about it.

He got down at Mandi House and the bus drove ahead, honking like a big bully. Nayan sat measuring the hurt she might have caused him. Salil met her again the next day to say that he was planning to travel with his friends from a theatre group. She did not say anything, had coffee sitting quietly, reading through Salil's book in the midst of his keyed-up friends. Samar was making ambitious but fatuous plans. The rest including Salil were listening with the gravest intent. She felt extremely tired.

And haven't I told you,
I hear your songs
As I walk through the dark woods
Of age
Alone and despondent
With thorns in my feet and
Thirst in my soul?
Didn't I tell you
I looked out of my window one day,
That half-rotten wooden frame,
One end of which hangs off its hinges...
And caught two cotton-clouds
Wandering gaily in the skies
Like strangers, they met
Shared some rain,
And drifted away
Each to its own den?
Did I not confess
We are still strangers
Very far from the phrase
I-understand-the-colours-on-your-face,
That we are still strangers
Still lonesome in a crowd
Not knowing what to talk 'bout
Apart from the weather

That we just hold on to silences
or meaningless chatter
That we don't yet know
How to hold the champagne flute
Or smoke in a classy manner?
We are still the same,
Raw and unproclaimed
But haven't I
Time and again tried to say
You look strangely familiar, girl
A familiar stranger,
Singing in my memories
As I walk the rail platforms
My bag slung on my shoulders
Not wanting you to come along,
But turning to hold that hand
In a babble of indifferent voices
Hopelessly waiting in vain
On the stations, in the woods,
In all my hideouts, in the rain.

A pack of lies indeed. Nayan thought, looking up from the book. She surveyed the faces at the table, comparing them with Salil's. Right now, they all seemed the same to her. She couldn't tell one from the other. She felt nervous and weary, seeing so many copies of the one she had believed was the only one for her.

Checkmate

Nayan rushed up the hospital stairs. A maze of corridors opened up before her. She nervously made her way through a herd of ward boys and nurses hurrying in all directions. The grey walls seemed like a pall of dank gloom. The rainstorm outside accentuated the claustrophobia indoors. Dark silhouettes of attendants sat on the benches lined outside the ICU. On one of those benches she found Jeeban sitting like another faceless silhouette, holding his head in his hands. Nayan touched his shoulder. He looked up at her helplessly.

Meera had fallen from the terrace stairs. With Jeeban in office the whole day, no one had been there to help. By the time Jeeban came home from press, Meera had lost consciousness; she lay beside a pool of blood that had dried up like a remorseless memory near the upturned wheelchair.

Jeeban had no clue how she had fallen. He was disconsolate. Nayan remembered, 'That slope, Jeeban.'

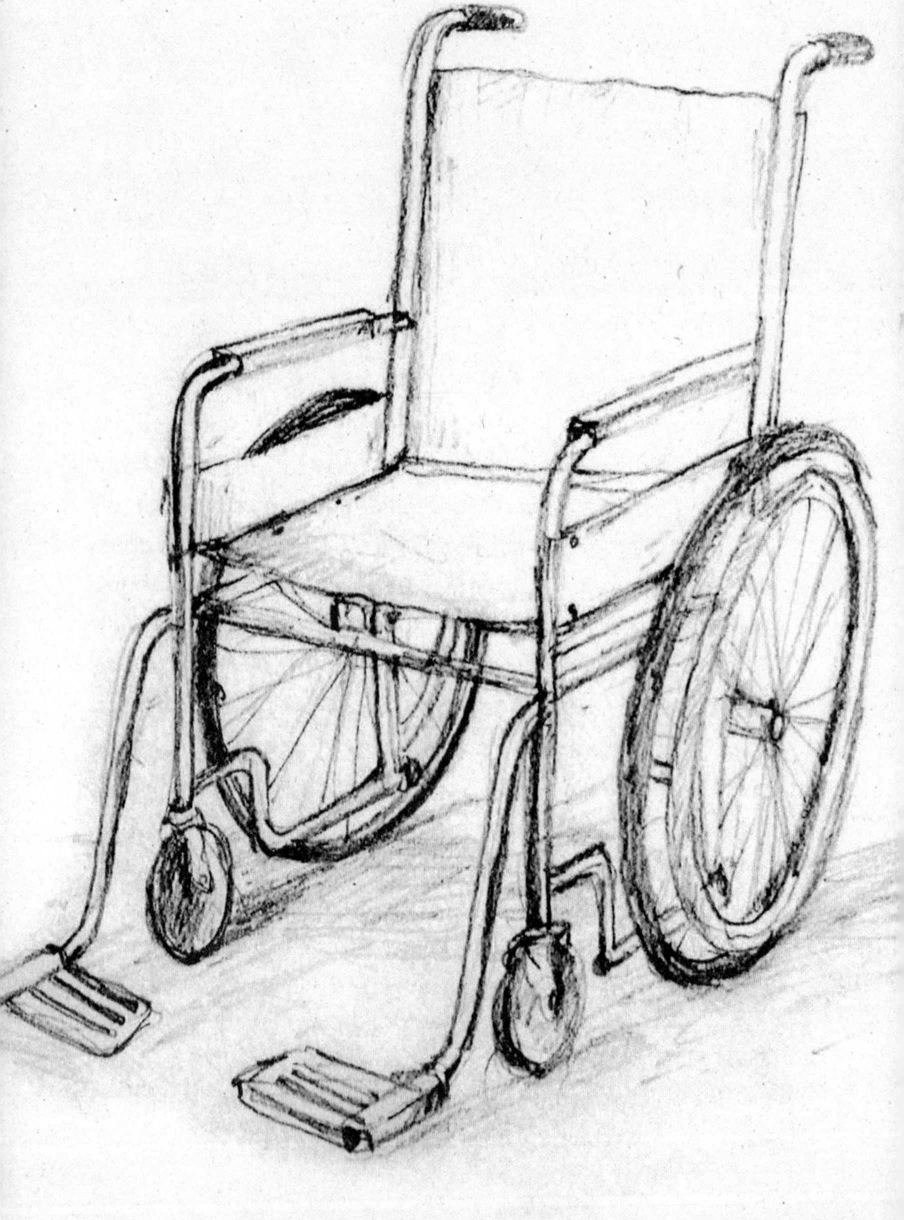

There was an inconspicuous little mound in the uneven floor on the terrace. After that it was an easy downward slope towards a long flight of stairs. Jeeban remembered how Nayan had tripped on her first visit to the house. She had said the slope was dicey and needed repair. Jeeban had noticed it then but forgotten about it later. That terrace was the best part of the house; more so after Jeeban had set up his exotic cacti garden up there. How much they had all loved the terrace. And Meera, she had loved it more than anyone else. That's where, under a tiled roof, she would paint every evening.

Jeeban and Nayan sat distraught. Jeeban's gaze was still fixed on the floor. People had walked across leaving behind wet footprints and slush from the roads as memories of their visit. Nayan felt nauseated by the smell she always associated with hospitals. She walked up to the only window at the end of the dark corridor and watched the rain pour down like white sheets outside. She tried to sketch Meera's face in the rain, see the water take her form.

A nurse came and handed Jeeban a see-through satchel that contained two gold bangles, a pair of earrings and a thin chain; they had been taken off Meera's body before her surgery began. Jeeban took out an earring and held it in the air, staring as if he were seeing it for the first time. The gold leaf that hung from a golden hook dangled a little in the stale, dispirited air.

After a few hours, the nurse walked up to them and told Jeeban something in a hushed voice. Jeeban got up, took Nayan by her arm and followed the nurse to the ICU. There, through the glass door, they saw Meera. Jeeban stuck his nose to the door, his grip tightening on Nayan. She lay on the bed surrounded by life-support gadgets. Jeeban's parents arrived shortly. Meera's family also rushed in. A whole group of Jeeban's colleagues and friends came by to ask after Meera. They all kept looking at her through the glass by turns till the nurse asked them to sit on the benches and wait.

Two days later, they were allowed to meet her after Jeeban noticed a tube inserted in a vein on her left wrist twitch slightly. They went in, two people at a time. Her face was contorted in agony. They came back sobbing silently to themselves.

Three more days passed in the same way. Neither did Meera open her eyes nor did the weather improve. It continued to drizzle all through. On the fifth day, Meera opened her eyes and the nurse called them inside, again two people at a time. Jeeban and Nayan went in. Meera's pain seemed to have subsided, but she looked extremely frail. She looked at Jeeban and smiled feebly.

'Don't checkmate me like that please,' Jeeban said, his voice breaking into a million shards.

An hour later, everyone was called inside. Jeeban sat quietly holding her hand, watching the nurse take out a tube from her nerve, another from under her nose. People sobbed softly around Meera.

Nayan stood near the window, watching the relentless drizzle wash the dirt off the black umbrellas and raincoats under which people stood huddled at bus stops. Traffic zoomed past them like a storm, splashing murky water from the road.

The world will pick up its pieces and walk again, but this time without Meera in its midst. Tears filled her eyes.

One last love story

Almost ten minutes had lapsed since Nayan rang the bell. She stood at the door, watching some potted plants wilt in the heat. She felt a little apprehensive, she didn't know why. It was just an uneasy feeling she had woken up with that morning. A hunch floating inside her, making her feel dizzy.

What was the matter? Why wasn't anyone answering the bell? She had spoken to the maid over the phone, who had confirmed the appointment after much reluctance, as was evident from the conversation in the background.

Harshini Deb, the legendary writer and poet, had turned reclusive and retired from literary and social circles for a decade now. She had isolated herself after suffering her first stroke at sixty. She lived alone in a flat, removed from the media and all the limelight she had received in the years when her novels fetched her award after award.

Now her publisher had brought out the twenty-fifth

edition of five of her novels. Nayan's editor had suggested she could try interviewing Harshini Deb and score a point over other news dailies that failed every time, saying she was a hard nut to crack. But here, no nut – hard or soft – seemed to be answering the door. It had been exactly fifteen minutes. Nayan was turning to leave when she heard a key turn inside a creaky lock. The handle pulled down with a rusty noise. Nayan wiped her feet on the doormat for the nth time and got ready to greet the hand that was unlocking the door. A middle-aged woman wearing a big golden stud in her nose took her inside and asked her to sit. It looked like a sitting-room-cum-study. The room was lined on three sides with shelves full of books. The fourth wall held citations and awards in a very dusty showcase.

Kitabon ki deevaron se
Inaamon ki kataaron se
Kabhi jee judati hun
toh kabhi jee churati hun...

(I console my heart sometimes
I shy away sometimes
From the walls of books
And rows of prizes)

So this is where those lines came from, Nayan thought, recalling a poem by Harshini Deb.

'Saanson ki panaahon se
Dhadkan ki sadaaon se
Kabhi main dil lagati hun
Kabhi daaman bachati hun'

(I serenade sometimes
And sometimes, I shrink away from
The shelter of breath
and the throbbing of my heart)

The maid emerged from another room and led her in. There, in the rectangular, dark room, Nayan saw someone sitting up in bed. The maid asked her to sit on a chair placed right next to the writer's bed. Harshini Deb sat with her back propped against an ivory pillow and her legs stretched out on the bed.

'Hello, Ms Deb!' Nayan said. 'I am Nayan from the *New Delhi Times*. Thank you for agreeing to this meeting.'

'I have not met journalists for years now. You were so persistent in your calls that I had to give in out of curiosity, you may say...'

'Thank you. I am really grateful, Ms Deb.'

'I hope you don't mind my sitting in bed. I can't move around much, you see... So you wanted an interview with me, Nayan. Is that it?'

'Yes.'

'I like your name. Simple, but can assume deeper meanings. Like, being Nayan, you can see the world better than the others... Things that others cannot perceive, can't read?'

Harshini Deb said, her sentences interrupted by prolonged pauses.

Nayan's eyes had adjusted to the lack of light inside the room by now. She could see more than just the writer's bony frame. Harshini Deb had big telling eyes above sunken cheeks. Her skin and lips had become flaky for want of care. Nayan could even see the veins in the writer's hands. She wore a purple batik kaftan. There was a gold chain strung with little pearls around her neck. She must have been a striking woman in her prime.

'Will you have tea?' the writer asked.

'Yes,' Nayan answered, 'if it isn't too much of a bother.'

Harshini Deb summoned the maid.

Nayan did not know where to begin. Though she knew the basic trick they had all been taught at work. Ask the first question, 'How did you become so and so?' and the celebrity will go on and on about it till you run out of recording time in your dictaphone or pages in your notebook. But this was the first time she was interviewing a writer. She was tongue-tied. To add to it, there was this inexplicable foreboding floating inside her, burgeoning into some unknown fear bit by bit. Fore-boding – Jugnu's letter came back to her, and she could not hear anything else. She strained her ears and tried to listen to what the maid was asking her. She was pouring out tea for them.

'How much sugar, didi?' she repeated.

Hearing came back to Nayan like a jolt. She replied, 'Just a single spoon.'

Harshini Deb took her cup and asked in a querulous voice, 'So, what is it? You look too quiet to become a reporter, child.

How old are you? Twenty-six, twenty-seven? Frightfully young, haan?'

Her question dissolved Nayan's clot, and switching her dictaphone on, she began: 'What were you like, Ms Deb, at my age?'

'Oh, that was so long ago. And yet to look at the past in another way makes all those fifty years seem like a speck in the universe of time. I have come a long way from there. Well, everybody does and does not. We tend to glorify our lives, our pains and our joys, give them too much importance perhaps. All of us. And I am no exception to the case.' She smiled.

'At your age, I had my first book published. A novella based on my mother's life. It was called *Yesterday*.The protagonist, newly-wed Keya, is a typical housewife, who begins her day offering prayers to the tulsi tree, going around it three times. She spends her day cooking, washing, cleaning and getting her husband Shyam babu's clothes ready for office. He is a clerk in the government registry office. She reads women's magazines in the afternoon. And at dusk she gets ready, carefully arranging the pleats of her starched sari and wearing jasmines in her hair before Shyam babu returns from work. One day, while cleaning Shyam babu's cupboard of old official files, she discovers a file full of letters. Reading them, she realizes they are from his first wife Mohua, whom he had abandoned and who still writes to him. The file also contains her medical reports from a mental asylum and letters from Mohua's brother writing about her illness. Mohua's letters to him contain vivid descriptions of her neurotic fantasies and nightmares. Keya packs her bags and leaves for Mohua's asylum and brings her home. She looks after Mohua for some years and returns to Shyam babu only after Mohua's death. Keya did what my mother did. It is a story of compassion and generosity and friendship between two women who share the same man, at least in theory. My mother developed a great bond with Mohua. In fact, in her last years, my mother was the only one Mohua trusted.'

Tea over, Nayan sat holding the empty cup in one hand and her dictaphone in the other. The writer continued to speak.

'Then between 1956 and '75 came several novels: *Everyday People, Joyce, By My Side, Mantu, Masterji and Meema, Mr Seth and the Master of Miscalculations, Warring Wives of Preetamgarh, A Bottle of Gin, Erring in America,* and so on...'

'Twenty-seven in all?' Nayan asked.

'Yes,' confirmed the writer. The maid came in again and said that it was time for her to leave.

'Isn't it a long day? Seems like I've been living through a whole life since morning.

Kuch ghanto mein jee rahi hun
Sari zindagi...
Har lamha, itihaas
Har pal, har ghadi...
Lagta hai aaj
Yeh antim adhyaay hoga...'

(I am living my whole life
In these few hours

Each moment writes its own history
Each second, every juncture
As though it will pen
The last chapter today…)

'What's the time?'

'It's one-thirty,' Nayan said, looking at her watch. Then she asked, 'Which novel of yours comes closest to your own story, Ms Deb?'

'Does anyone or anything come truly close to being you? Possibly not…

What remembrance there is
For me to lean on,
To swim to,
To hold on to
In the quiet, cold violence of
The sea of separation…
That afternoon – yes!
Us dancing to
'Strangers in the night',
Now sitting down
Then gasping,
Now laughing
Then, tears rollin' down our eyes,
We opened a bottle of gin
Lying by our side…

'Yes, one could appropriate one's life into fiction. There can be approximations and also endless futile speculations by your reader whose personal story your novel becomes in the end...'

'Why gin? Anything special about the drink?'

'Too many questions, beta. Too many you ask me today...' The writer sounded slightly disoriented now.

Nayan realized that it was a very silly thing to ask – why only gin!

'But I quite like them... your questions... At least you are not asking me how-did-you-feel-when-you-got-this-award or how-did-you-feel-about-not-getting-that-year's-literary-award. Oh, how sick such queries make me!

'Gin. Because it's my favourite drink. And because it reminds me of some beautiful moments of togetherness and solitude. Family, friends and being with myself.' She paused and took a deep breath. Then she asked Nayan, 'What day is it today?' and turned to look at the calendar on her side table.

'It's Sunday,' Nayan said.

'Sunday, again. Then, I'll treat you to some gin if you like. My throat's parched. But you will have to help me a bit, beta.'

Nayan said, 'Don't bother, Ms Deb. It's perfectly all right. Just tell me where it is kept.'

'The bottle and glasses are kept there on that shelf in the sitting room, on the left-hand side right next to the kitchen. And you'll find tonic water in the fridge there.'

Nayan fetched everything.

'Please get sliced lemon, too, from the fridge. Jyoti must

have kept them in there. And get an ice-tray too from the deep freeze, beta,' the writer said, sounding faint.

When everything was ready, the writer told Nayan how much gin to pour into the glasses, how much tonic water to add and how to arrange a thin slice of lime on the brim of the glasses. Their drinks were fixed.

Nayan didn't knew what to make of it. This woman who had not met any outsider for years had all of a sudden agreed to talk, and was offering a reporter a drink. It was strange.

'If you don't mind my asking, why do you live alone? Don't you have a family?' Nayan asked, picking up her glass.

'I don't live alone. I live with myself, beta. It's difficult only because I can hardly move about. It's painful for me, getting up from the bed, washing and all. Otherwise, I quite like being on my own. Yes, I have a family. My husband died five years ago. Mihir Deb. You must know his name. He was a historian. My son lives in Minnesota in the United States. He's a mathematician. He has married a Parsi girl who teaches in the same university as him. I have a daughter who lives in Bombay. She is working with Life India Insurance and is married to a boy who works with the Reserve Bank. She comes down every few months to see me. My son also comes once in two years. I live here because I have lived here most of my life, because my husband lived here, and because I want to die here and nowhere else.

'I was twenty-three when I got married. My husband was the same age. He was an extraordinary student and three years later, he became a lecturer. We would travel in and outside India for lectures and conferences. He would get busy with work and I would explore new places by myself. I met many people then. But gradually, sitting idle for days began to make me irritable and grumpy. That's when Mihir suggested that I write about what I saw on these journeys with him. I began writing the things I saw on our travels, about people I met. Then one day, it struck me that I could write my mother's story. That's when Keya and Mohua happened to me. I wrote *Yesterday*. It got published episodically in one of Mihir's friend's weekly magazines. It was well received and later published as a novella along with three short stories based on my travels through South-east Asia with Mihir.

'I wrote most of *Joyce, By My Side* during the time I was expecting my son. We lived in Trinidad for those three years, Mihir and I. Mihir was teaching a module on medieval Indian history. There I met Joyce, a Carribean girl. She was twenty then. Deaf and dumb. But it was amazing, the way she understood things and communicated with people. She came asking for work and stayed on those three years, helping me with house work and everything else. She took very good care of my son when he was born. She came to India with us and decided to settle here for the rest of her life. She went back to her country three years ago, when her niece came to take her away. That novel is a dialogue between someone like me and someone who doesn't have a voice, nor hearing, set in the Carribean.

'Abhay, my son, wouldn't go to sleep without listening to a story. He grew up demanding more and more stories and fairytales from me. I wrote *Mantu, Masterji and Meema* on life in boarding schools for him when he was twelve. *Mr Seth and*

Master of Miscalculations came when Abhay and Archana, my daughter, reached high school. It was a funny story about a gawky young man, Sujal Seth, who gets a job as an accountant in a sarkari bank; it's also a satire on how the Indian government functioned under Indira Gandhi in the '70s. *Warring Wives of Preetamgarh* came much later. It was about the women of a small district in Rajasthan picking up guns against feudalistic chauvinism.'

Harshini exhaled then and said, 'And so and so forth…'

The dictaphone sounded shut and Nayan turned the side of the cassette. She said: 'You didn't write for some nine years. This was after *Don't Err in America* came out, between 1970 and 1979, after which came your first poetry collection, *Poet's Court*. Why such a gap for a prolific writer like you who had written fifteen novels in a span of twelve years?'

'Have you read that one?' Harshini Deb asked, looking intently into her glass of gin.

'In fact, Ms Deb, that's my favourite of the five collections I have read. I like it the best. It was only yesterday, when I researched your career graph on the Internet, that I came to know of this long gap. But you just mentioned a title I don't know of. What was it…? Ah, yes, *The Colour of Noon*…? I did not find the name in the list of your books.'

'You are very inquisitive, beta…' She sounded tired. 'Let me fix myself another drink. I will not offer you more because you might have to get back to work…'

'There must be something about the gap which made you write poetry like that. You hadn't written poetry before that. In fact, that voice is very different from the ones in your novels,' Nayan said looking at her. 'They're written in such a masked, cryptic way that it's difficult to discern much about your predicament from them.'

'Holi, do you like playing holi?' she asked Nayan, as though she were asking the whole room, its walls and furniture. '1971. Jaya begins her day preparing for Holi. She makes sweets, gujias and other goodies for the guests, tidies up the house for a get-together and listens with contentment to her four-year-old twin sons yell and sing songs while playing with pichkaaris on the terrace. Her husband, an air force pilot posted in Jammu, is due to come home by afternoon for the festival. She waits, happily thinking of him and her kids. Just then, she hears a song from an old Hindi film, coming from a tea stall on the roadside. She had heard this song on Holi, years ago in college. She remembers…

'Jenny, Jeet, Vikram, Shashi, Alec, Aditi, Subrat and others dancing in a frenzy in the college field. Their faces are unrecognizable in mottled blues, greens, pinks, a scary silver and a monster black. Only their teeth shine like pearls in the sun. Their bhaang-induced laughter annoys the principal, Mohanty, who sits listening to the radio inside his residence on the campus. In the midst of festivity, sits Lenin, on the raised parapet outside the classrooms, smoking a joint and looking on like a detached witness. They called him Lenin in college. His real name is Jatin, Jaya recalls. How does it matter now that he's not here? When the dancing stops, and they sit down on the ground, cracking jokes, eating gulabjamuns laced with bhaang and humming songs, Lenin gets up, crushing the cigarette stub under his feet, takes a little pink colour from a heap of gulal on the parapet, smears it with his coarse hands all over Jaya's soft face and asks everyone to dance again. The group gets up and starts dancing afresh.

'How does it matter today? Why does it have to, after all these years? Jaya keeps asking herself, moving about the house as she prepares for the party – a long planned reunion of old college friends. The phone rings. The caller asks for Jaya Sehgal. She confirms it's her, accepts Holi greetings and hangs up.

'Last day of college... She remembers him talking about it all. Revolution and societal change. He looks worn but resolute. His eyes look deeper and bloodshot. He asks her whether she will go with him. He says it's his passion, and he has to go with or without her. She says she can't. They enter the convocation hall wearing their black robes. He moves to the left to join the boys, she walks to the right to sit with the girls. Three years later, she becomes a clinical psychologist. Jenny marries a rich man. Jeet takes on his father's tyre business. Aditi joins Hindustan Lever as a corporate executive. Alec joins the civil services. Subrat dies in a car crash. Vikram goes to England to study law and Shashi joins the air force.'

Nayan interrupted at this point, 'And Lenin?'

Harshini Deb put her glass back on the table and answered, 'He goes to West Bengal with Sharat da, a senior from college. They say he became a Naxalite.'

She continued, 'But why today of all days? Why has he come in like an aching easterly on a day like this? She had waited for him for two years, saying no to Shashi's advances. But in the end, she gave in. Tired of the loneliness and of Lenin's memories, she settled for someone who loved her even though she didn't until many years later.

'The phone rings again. It's Vikram this time, calling to greet her. He asks about Shashi and whether he's coming in the evening. They talk about his wife and work and the call ends.

'Yes. She thinks, she didn't love Shashi then but now it's different. She knows it is the companionship she values, a deep sense of comfort, warmth, friendship, gratitude and trust. Yes, it's about faith, her marriage to Shashi. And that, she thinks, is reason enough to think this is love.'

The writer stopped. She looked tired and washed out. Then she asked Nayan to open a cupboard and take out a tattered album that sat on files full of old papers. Nayan pulled it out and Harshini Deb placed it on her lap. Nayan felt a little tired too. Dizzy with the afternoon heat, yet interested in the tale. 'What happened after that?' she asked the writer.

'The day rolls on. By noon the kids are tired of playing with colours. Jaya runs them a bath, scrubbing the colours off their bodies, and puts them in bed. She arranges fresh flowers in the vases and splashes them with cold water to keep them from drooping. Then she waits for her guests, filling her time with trivial thoughts. Which sari she should wear. Pink on white? Lenin's favourite colours. Then she puts dry colours in brass bowls out in the courtyard and lines up the music for the party.

'Around four Shashi returns. Guests start coming in after

five. Jeet arrives first, carrying a bottle of expensive champagne in one hand followed by an assistant carrying several boxes of sweets. Then the others: Aditi, her husband and six-year-old daughter, and some other batchmates. Alec arrives after six, late as usual. He jokes around in the same old manner. Jaya fetches snacks while they recline chit-chatting, exchanging updates on each other's lives. Vikram arrives around half past seven announcing, 'Surprise, surprise!' All eyes turn towards the door. And the 'Naxalite', a limping Lenin, enters to everybody's shock. It's Shashi who dissolves the silence with a loud 'hello'. Old friends welcome him, hug him, half dazed and half elated to see him back in their world.

'Only Jaya does not know what to do, or how to react. She stands where she was a moment ago, near the coffee table arranging snacks, looking at him, a frozen well of sorrow melting inside her. She is amazed at how her world has changed in a blink.

'The friends move out into the courtyard. They tap their feet to music and play with colours. It's like the old days. Gradually, as the evening progresses, they begin dancing, a jovial Vikram taking the lead. Amidst laughter and music, Jaya stands in one corner, angry with herself for being so affected by Lenin's sudden return. Lenin gets up and tries shaking a leg too. He looks weak, very weak, but energetic and eccentric still. The dancing continues. Lenin moves out of the circle. Picking up a pinch of gulal from a brass bowl, he crosses the courtyard and, walking up to Jaya, smears the colour on her cheeks, saying, 'I'm back. How have you been, Jaya?'

The writer was silent for a few minutes, her face turned downwards. When she looked up again, her face appeared clam. The wrinkles on her face seemed settled and even.

Then she said, 'A lot had changed since Holi that afternoon, years ago in college, to this afternoon of surprise, a comeback.'

Harshini Deb put down her glass which was empty now.

Nayan looked at her. Her eyes had a strange spark in them.

'Nayan, you asked me a question when you came in. I have answered it.'

She paused a little and continued, 'For these last seven or eight years, I have been alone, very lonely, especially after Mihir passed away. I don't remember the last time I talked to someone at this length. I think you have come for some purpose, but I don't know what.'

'Of course, I came here to interview you,' Nayan said.

'Oh yes. That I remember. I am talking of a deeper purpose. Why today, why you, such a young girl... on this hot afternoon... to share gin and tonic with me. Why? Anyway, let these puzzles be. Let me give you something. Keep it carefully. I am giving you my last work.' She picked up a file full of stapled sheets from beside her pillow and gave it to Nayan.

Nayan looked at her questioningly.

'This is my last novel, *The Colour of Noon*. Keep it with you. I won't be writing any more.'

Nayan didn't know what to say, how to react. 'How can I keep this? I will read it and return it to you,' she said.

'No, it's for you. You keep it. My gift to you for giving me company all this while.' She laughed a guttural laugh.

Nayan stood confused for some time. Then she began picking up the glasses and the gin bottle.

'I'll put them back in the kitchen before I leave,' she said.

'No, leave them here. It's very hot today. I will drink some more. You may leave now. You must be getting late. Goodbye and God bless you.'

Nayan picked up her bag and dropped the dictaphone into it. Holding the file in one hand, she turned to leave. Before closing the door behind her back, she turned and asked, 'What will you do now, after I leave, Ms Deb?'

'Who, me? I think I'll flip through this old album,' she said, a bright smile forming at the curve of her lips, 'looking at Alec, Aditi, Vikram, Jeet, Subrat, Jenny, Shashi and Lenin…'

Two days later, while Nayan was furiously typing out a story that had to go to print that evening, Hari came and patted her on the back. 'Good job, girl! Keep at it. Hard work pays.'

'Please, Hari, give me two minutes. We'll talk then.'

'By the way, did you interview that writer you were talking about?'

'Yes. But why do you ask? Not planning to steal my beat are you?' Nayan asked dryly.

'No, man, just asking because if you haven't, you've missed the boat and the only thing you will get to write about her now is her obit.'

Nayan swirled around in her chair.

'She was found dead last evening by her maid, but the news

wasn't reported till this evening when her daughter flew down to Delhi.'

Nayan's hands shook. She rummaged through her bag and took out her phone diary. She called Harshini Deb's residence. Her daughter answered the call and said her mother had died in her sleep the previous night.

Nayan left for home immediately, sobbing and shivering all the way. She stayed up all night reading through the manuscript the writer had given her. Next afternoon in office, she was asked to write a half-page obituary to be published with the last interview she had given. Nayan played back the dictaphone. The tape had ended just before Harshini Deb began talking about her last novel.

Wandering in the delirious nerve

Nayan continued to think of Salil. She heard from his friends about the failure of their street theatre venture. She waited to hear from him. Her friends from Gandharva, school friends, batchmates from university and colleagues at work had gradually begun to get married or engaged one by one. She grew lonelier as one friend after another turned into part of a couple and got absorbed in their own lives. She withdrew to the periphery of the shared circle and plunged into her music.

At times, finishing work early and not knowing what to do next, she would go to a coffee shop. Ordering an Irish coffee, she would sit for hours on end, scribbling mindlessly on paper napkins.

Or, she would step out of office, climb up the pedestrian overbridge on the Bahadur Shah Zafar Marg crossing near ITO, and stand there for a long time, just watching the city gush past

under her feet, looking like a fluid cavalcade of yellow, green, red and orange headlights and tail lights.

At home, things had started falling into place. Ratri had decided to teach music to children. A neat little signage for her school had gone up near the gate and the guest room where Guruji had given her his last lessons had been set up for her students. Tarun had finally achieved a breakthrough in his research. His team had succeeded in mapping the gene that proved that certain kinds of cancers were hereditary and familial in nature. His photos and interviews were appearing all over the media. Neel had written to Ratri telling her that he had decided to get married and was coming home soon on a long holiday. The letter also had a photo attached to it. It was Gehna's. So, Ratri had wedding plans, too, to keep her busy. Mrs Singh, after eight years of self-imposed exile, had invited friends from the neighbourhood for a prayer service on Jugnu's twenty-ninth birth anniversary. Nayan helped her prepare for the get-together. She also convinced Mrs Singh to unlock Jugnu's room and have it cleaned up and aired.

Over a year and a half had passed since Meera's death. Jeeban had become unusually quiet, and mostly stayed home after work. Nayan occasionally went to see him with homemade food. She'd lay the table on Meera's favourite terrace on which bright cacti flowers were in full bloom that year. Often they would go out for a drive to India Gate. They would drive through Lutyens's Delhi, and go round and round, watching couples, families, louts eating ice-cream and walking under the massive orange floodlights.

One such evening, a few months later, they talked about their lives. And how their loneliness had started eating into their mind and body. Like a peepal tree that appears from nowhere and sends down twisted roots through a crack in a building. Jeeban wept openly for the first time, for Meera; the emptiness in his life was driving him insane. Nayan affirmed how difficult it was to go on living; living and not living, just going through the ritual of life.

It seemed unreal and selfish perhaps, specially keeping the past in mind, that they should think like this now. And yet, how small and humanly real they had become in love; they had become disconsolately, unabashedly alone, seeking the warmth of unconditional friendship to save themselves. A companionship that could pull the blinds down on their lonesome lives. Too much time on their hands scared them now. They had forgotten what to do with it. It was as if it had grown fangs and chased them from one end of their minds to the other end of their bodies. On the other hand, life had made it really simple for them; it had reduced their choices impossibly. They wanted a friend, to drink their morning tea with, to discuss the daily newspaper with, to decide what plants needed to be bought, to just hear somebody talk incessantly so that the silences on the walls of their houses would not come down and walk all over them, so that the turgid moss of sorrow in the air around them could be washed away with words.

When Jeeban said, who knew better than her what their lives were like and how they needed to be saved from themselves – it did not startle her. It did not shock her to hear Jeeban say that they should probably think of getting together someday. Because she knew what Meera had meant to him and what they were going through.

When she got down from his car in front of her house that evening, a tacit understanding shone between them in the moonlight. As she entered her house, she thought of one more reason for going ahead and saying yes; a revenge against Salil for the way he was. He needed to be punished for being Salil. She would show him that she could get married to someone else and still find happiness. She knew it would cause him much hurt, however carefree he appeared to be.

They did not love each other, Jeeban and she. If there was a reason strong enough to go ahead with it, it was affection, old familiarity, acceptance of each other's minds, and indomitable trust.

Still, it was difficult for her to imagine getting married to Jeeban. This was not how she had imagined her life would pan out. Jeeban was a constant in her life, like her mother in a way. In fact, he was the only friend since college whom she could lean on. In contrast to her equation with Salil, her association with Jeeban had been rational, simple and placid all through.

She did not mention it to her mother. Ratri was busy talking to her father about Neel's wedding to Gehna. Nayan wanted to first sort it out within herself. Also, she had some time. Jeeban had said they could think it over another six months.

A secret monologue in fresh orange juice

Neel married Gehna in Kolkata in her father's house. The newly-weds were received by Ratri, Tarun, Nayan and others in the family. Palash came down to stay in Delhi with Gehna and Neel for a few days. Gehna was a little less uncomfortable, having him around. Maybe she had forgiven him.

That year was a busy one for Nayan. She travelled out of town for concerts more than usual. She had also said yes to marrying Jeeban. Harshini Deb's last novel, which the writer had gifted her, was on the stands, after going through numerous rounds of scrutiny in order to verify that the manuscript was actually hers.

As for Salil, she had heard nothing from him or of him for over a year now. Sometimes she wondered whether he had ever existed in her life. What if he had been a figment of her imagination. With Jeeban, she knew everything was real and

tangible. His presence, his affection and his understanding. They were to marry soon, but it still felt strange. At times she felt as if she was intruding on Jeeban's life, his past with Meera, his memories of Meera, even though she wasn't around any more. She thought she was trespassing on a world that Jeeban and Meera had created for themselves, and which belonged only to the two of them.

Besides, the idea of marriage itself seemed unbelievable; even after closely watching Neel and Gehna tie the knot. Whenever she went to fetch anything from Ratri's dresser, she would look hard in the mirror. Then, pulling one of the many red bindis stuck on its frame, she would stick it on her forehead and gape at the face in the mirror with disbelief, as if it were not hers.

One such day, Jeeban caught up with her on his way home from work and drove her to a coffee bar. The coffee bar was glowing with tiny blue and red square lamps. It was full of youngsters chit-chatting away over steaming mugs of coffee, sugar-coated doughnuts, muffins crowned with blueberry sauce or hot chocolate and grilled lemon chicken sandwiches. Ordering two espressos, Jeeban and Nayan sat looking around at the couples and groups, soaking in the hubbub of that atmosphere. When their coffee mugs arrived, they slowly drank from them, discussing the most suitable dinner for a cool rainy evening like this. Mutton cooked in garam masala and pure ghee with plain rice and a simple yoghurt and onion salad.

Before leaving, Nayan insisted, 'Wait. I'll pay the bill.'

'As you wish,' said Jeeban.

'But you will cook the mutton for dinner,' Nayan added with a smile.

'As you wish, again.'

But as she rummaged her bag for her wallet, her hand fell on a slip of paper, a receipt really. She pulled it out along with the wallet.

Handing the wallet to Jeeban she said, 'Please go and pay, Jeeban.'

She unfolded the slip and started reading.

> 'Thus,
> Sat two mad souls
> Slurping stale coffee
> In a mad mad coffee house
> Thinking it was tea!'

> That delirious nerve
> You wander to
> In the middle of a conversation
> Take me to that invisible city
> In your mind
> Will you...?'

'What's that?' Jeeban asked. 'Don't tell me you're checking your old coffee bills, you stingy woman!'

Nayan's voice choked. 'Just some paper. It's nothing... Let's go.'

'Yes,' Jeeban said, 'let's, 'cause I'm the one who's supposed to be cooking dinner tonight.'

That night Nayan dipped her pen in orange juice and wrote,

'I was thinking of Meera, walking around in the house while Jeeban was cooking. He stood in the kitchen humming one of Meera's favourite oldies. Her absence intensifies her presence around us. She is everywhere, her imprint on every little thing in the house. Jeeban's chessboard lies covered in dust on the coffee table, every piece intact, pawns frozen in positions where Meera had left their last game unfinished. Meera's paintings fill almost every inch on the walls. Her things are neatly kept, the way she did. The rugs, the bookshelves, the bone-china teacups, the unchanged calendar in the hall – everything conceivable in that house reminds me of her. I remember them setting up the house before they got married. A thin duvet and pillow lie on the sofa in front of the TV. Jeeban sleeps outside, in the sitting room; he can't bear to sleep in their bedroom any more. The house has turned into a museum of Meera's belongings; why, Jeeban himself is one of them. He belonged to Meera. He will always belong with her. One can see the mute desperation in him to preserve what he had shared with her. And that disintegrates him bit by bit each day. We need to save each other. We need to salvage ourselves from this slow-setting death.'

Remember?

Salil returned one day, his green and steel mouth organ shining in his shirt pocket, his hair overgrown and dishevelled, hanging like an awning over his eyebrows. He had become very dark and thin, and so Nayan didn't wonder why he looked even taller than before. He came holding a long-stemmed white lily, silent and sober, and waited outside her house till she emerged, ready for office.

Nayan would have walked straight ahead and past him; she was not expecting him. The way he was looking, she could have easily missed him. Except that she couldn't miss his eyes. She knew those eyes too well.

She stopped. Salil said, 'Hi, I'm Salil, you remember?', giving her the lily.

'Since when have you started buying flowers for women?' Nayan asked, scathingly.

'Since the day I fell for the woman who stands behind the counter at the florist's!'

Nayan laughed and said, 'So you have become old and clichéd after all. So much for your bohemianism, haan?'

They walked to the bus stop. When they were inside a bus, Salil said, 'Wait, I'll get the tickets.'

Nayan was surprised. 'What makes you so chivalrous out of the blue? I have always paid for all our tickets and coffee and tea.'

He laughed. And Nayan laughed too. At herself. Since when had she become so acerbic, so bitter?

'How's Jeeban? I've got him some very good cigars from Burma?'

'He's fine.' Then everything came back to her like a deluge. Her decision to marry Jeeban. Meera's death. The trauma that followed. Salil didn't know any of that.

She answered again, 'He's fine.'

Then she asked him, 'When did you go to Burma?'

'You know about my trip to West Bengal with my friends, right? Our street theatre project did not do wonders though. *Box office par baat nahin bani*. So, we decided to go travel around after making some money doing odd jobs. I took up a job at the government handicraft expo, where they sell these giant sculptures, antique furniture, handicraft from various states at exorbitant prices. I also worked in a bookstall, at a coffee house, even in a primary healthcare centre in the Sundarbans. And then around June last year, I went to Nepal, Bhutan, Burma and Tibet with my gang.'

Nayan couldn't hear a word. All she could think of was that she was marrying Jeeban. Meera was dead. And Salil didn't know.

Salil realized she was not listening. He stopped talking and looked out at the black clouds coming their way from afar in the skies.

After some time he asked, 'How's Meera? I'd like to see her new paintings. Did she hold any more exhibitions after I left? You know, you might find it strange, because I also felt so, but I dreamt of her two years ago when I was in Murshidabad with my friends. Meera stood on that terrace of their house, painting a canvas on the easel. And Jeeban's cacti had a million flowers. Nayan, I saw Meera standing.'

Nayan gulped. 'Salil, Meera died two years ago. She died of a head injury. Her wheelchair rolled down that very terrace while Jeeban was away at work.'

An opaque sheet of silence settled on them. The bus reached a stop near Nayan's office. They got down, inching their way through the crowd crammed inside.

'Jeeban's gone to Jaipur for some work. He'll be back tomorrow,' she told him, standing near the gate to her office.

'Okay, then I'll meet up some old friends and my publisher. You finish work and I shall see you here in the evening,' he said and turned to go.

And I am marrying Jeeban, Salil.

No, she hadn't told him this. She wanted to say, 'Don't come back, Salil. Please don't. If you do, I'll have to tell you I am marrying Jeeban.'

Around eight in the evening, when she stepped out of office, Salil stood waving at her from a cigarette shop across the road. They went up the footbridge and stood in the middle of it for a while, looking at the traffic flying beneath and across. Coming down the bridge, they walked for another half hour till they were tired and Nayan suggested they take a bus home.

After dinner with Ratri and her, Salil left saying he would meet her again.

Ratri handed Nayan a glass of warm milk after dinner. 'Do you want to marry him? I mean, I quite like him minus his long hair and even longer absences. And that book,' she said, pointing to one kept atop a pile on Nayan's desk, 'I like it too. He's sensitive. What does he do?'

'No, I don't want to marry him, Ma.'

'But you should think of getting married now. Your grandpa has written to me from Kalchini. He has asked whether you want to get married now that Neel's married. Take your time, but I want to you to marry someone who has enough time to build a life with you…'

Instead, I am planning to marry Jeeban, Nayan thought. She said, 'Please, Ma. I'll tell you when I'm sure I want to marry. You're right, Salil has no time for me. He can't share his time with me. His time bends or expands for him as he pleases. His time is much longer than mine, and far nimbler. And my time seems to have become locked inside his stopped wrist watch forever. Like yours in Pa's, perhaps…'

She thought she should have told her mother. She had the

right to know. And Salil, too. That she was marrying Jeeban. But it wasn't that simple. The telling.

Salil and she, they had not even done the first round of confessing that they loved each other. She traced in her mind the times they had spent in his studio painting it, preparing it for the sale of artifacts he and his friends made, the times they had been happiest together and the times they had chosen to overlook each other – they had never talked of love or how much or how little they cared. They had just lived it, been through it without feeling the need.

She pulled out her copy of *Divan-e-Ghalib* from a shelf and began to read in a glassy voice. The words swayed in the filigreed light of the cane lamp swinging over her bed.

> *'Khuda ke vaaste abhi parda na Kaabe se utha, zaalim*
> *Kahin aisa na ho yahaan bhi wohi kaafir sanam nikle'*
>
> (For God's sake don't lift the veil off the Kaaba
> The infidel inside might just turn out to be my
> lover)

Salil had impeccable diction, and a voice that felt words, that glorified them just by touching them. Words turned into little jewels when embraced by his voice. Listening to him read poetry was like going on a night safari. New meanings were sighted as silent but sudden discoveries. Realizations dawned slowly like quiet thrills; they lit up one by one, and then in whole constellations, like stars in the deep purple evening sky. Everyone who knew Salil and liked poetry, wanted to be read to by him. She continued to read, turning pages at random.

'Qaasid ke aate-aate khat ek aur likh rakhun
Main jaanta hun joh woh likhenge jawab mein'

(Let me write another letter before the messenger
arrives
For I know what she will write in reply)

Salil's voice spoke in her ears as she read on.

'Mat pooch ke kya haal hai mera tere peeche
Tu dekh ke kya rang hai mera tere aage'

(Don't ask after me while you are far
Watch the colour of my face while you are near)

Lying down in bed, she pulled up the duvet to cover her knees, closed her eyes and began humming.

'Dil hi toh hai, na sang-o-khisht, dard se bhar na aaye kyun
Royenge hum hazaar baar koi hamein sataaye kyun...'

(It's merely a heart, not stone or brick, why
shouldn't it fill with pain?
I shall cry a thousand times, why should anyone
trouble me so...?)

At Jeeban's house the next evening, she sat watching the two men talk. Jeeban gave him suggestions for his next book. It was going to be a novel, Salil said. Nayan had made a resolve, but there was something that rankled in her mind still. Her discomfort in the presence of Jeeban and Salil together annoyed her. Jeeban's behaviour was completely normal with Salil. The surprise that he expressed on seeing him was purely that of an unexpected delight. He looked unmoved and unperturbed otherwise. He barely discussed Meera with Salil except when the latter said he was sorry to hear about her... He always held his emotions tightly in control. Salil was so different from him, quiet and watery eyed when hurt, volatile and unconvincingly loud and snappy when angry. She sat observing the two of them, almost comparing them on every count. They were busy trying out the new cigars now. Jeeban's composure told her that he trusted her, and that she was free to do whatever she wanted.

With Salil, she felt it was so much more mystical, so surreal, like a dream. A dream that never quite left her, that kept returning. Like a leaf that wafts between the tree branch and earth in a feeble breeze, not wanting to fall. But, she knew, it was time the leaf fell. It was time the dream died.

Two cigarettes and the unfinished minar

The next day, a little before dusk, Salil and Nayan sat inside the Qutab complex near the second unfinished Alai Minar. Salil said he was going home to meet his parents. They sat looking at tourists who were clicking photographs of Qutab Minar and of themselves against it.

'Nayan,' he said, 'will you smoke a cigarette with me? Not that I want you to ruin your voice, but because I want you to share this one little sin with me. I want us to be partners in crime, you know. So that you know why I go on smoking endlessly. Remember, you had asked me once and you never got an answer from me?'

Nayan laughed a wry laugh. She pulled out a cigarette from the pack Salil held out to her. He lit a matchstick. Holding the cigarette between her lips, Nayan brought it close to the flame, inhaled, and the cigarette lit up.

'You want me to ruin my voice, haan?'

He didn't answer.

The smoke went up her nose and Nayan choked. She laughed when the coughing subsided. Her laughter sounded hollow, it seemed to come from a dark cavern inside her. She inhaled again, looking at him, and laughed again. Her eyes changed then. She looked up at the uneven mound of red sandstones lying on the broad tip of the unfinished minar's edge. How hopelessly incomplete and estranged from its surroundings it looked. Without the pigeons circling round it today, it looked lonesome and ruinous. Tears rolled down and stopped on her lips. The kohl rimming her eyes melted and got smudged. She shut her eyes, her face still turned up.

The cigarette stood stiff between her fingers. Ash accumulated on its burning end. Salil's gaze lingered on the teardrops. They were glistening on her lips. She was so quiet, her lips didn't quiver when she cried. The tears didn't lose shape. They just sat there touching her lips, in complete awe of them. They sat there as though learning from her a lesson in patience and forgetting, in love and acceptance. She looked incomparably beautiful right now. The kohl in her eyes had spread to become a shadow of itself. He could go on looking at her like this forever. He exhaled and a cloud of grey smoke escaped his mouth. 'Here come the birds!' he said.

A flock of pigeons came swooping from beyond the skies perhaps and began circling the minar. Nayan opened her eyes and a gentle smile rippled across her mouth. One last drop of tear rolled down her cheek. Laughing, she said, 'So wizardry is your next big project, is it?'

Salil laughed. Then they laughed together. The pigeons went racing, flapping their wings endlessly, around the incomplete minar, chirping loudly.

'You must have your prize then,' said Nayan. She handed the cigarette to Salil and took out a big envelope from her bag. 'There you are!'

Salil looked puzzled.

'Letters. For you. Open it when it's over,' she said, a smile, somewhat shrewd, waking on her lips.

'What? The cigarette?' Salil asked, sniggering and crushing his cigarette beneath his feet.

'No. When I'm gone.'

She took her cigarette from his hand, smoked it one last time, and crushed it beneath her feet like him, stamping her chappals this way and that in a little arc.

'That's how you do it, haan?' she asked.

Dusk fell. She said, 'Stay well, Salil. And safe journey. I have to go home now.' She looked at him for a long moment, took in those eyes, which reminded her of a lake lapping at the edges of an old fortress. Then, she turned and left.

Salil bent over, picked up Nayan's crushed cigarette butt from the ground, and put it in his shirt pocket.

Us together by the river

They were to get married in Benares. Jeeban accompanied her to the music festival in the holy city. She was going to perform there in place of Ratri. She suggested they could get married there. One day after the festival ended, they met a pundit. The pundit looked at his patra, his scroll of time, dates and planetary positions, and suggested an auspicious hour after nine in the night.

Jeeban stood waiting in the hotel lounge when Nayan came down from her room dressed in an off-white and red Benaresi silk sari and Ratri's wedding jewellery that she had brought along to wear to the concert. He said: 'You look just the way you looked at my wedding with Meera.'

'Yes, only a little older now,' replied Nayan.

'Just a little bit,' said Jeeban.

'Shall we leave? We'll reach just in time for the aarti and then wait for the pundit to arrive.' Jeeban stretched his hand towards her.

Nayan took his hand and nodded. His eyes shone with the protective affection he had always had for her.

Dashashwamedha Ghat was not very far from the hotel. They began walking down through the peopled lanes that led to the ghat. They stopped on their way at a tea stall and Jeeban suggested, 'Let's have a nice cup of elaichi tea before we proceed.'

As they drank tea, Nayan thought she heard Salil's voice speak to her:

> 'Thus
> Two mad souls
> Sat slurping stale coffee
> In a mad mad coffee house
> Thinking it was tea!'

They threw the mud kullarhs into an overflowing wastebasket and started walking again.

Nayan looked at Jeeban. He appeared very calm. He took out a cigarette from his pocket and struck a match to light it. Nayan thought of their days in college and remembered how they had started as friends... no, not as friends. Like other juniors in college, she too had been in awe of Jeeban, the super dynamic, brash and well-read senior. Even Jugnu used to hero-worship him in a way, although they were batchmates.

Deepesh, her boyfriend, always looked insecure around him. Where had all those people gone? Deepesh had been packed off to America by his parents after Jugnu's suicide. How would she have reacted if she knew Nayan was about to marry Jeeban? Jugnu, I'm getting married, she thought.

The sun went down and the lights came on one by one in the array of shops in the lane. Nayan halted at a kiosk selling vermillion in wooden caskets. An old woman and a blind young girl were sitting inside the stall. They sat lost in their thoughts, crooning some folk tune. Jeeban had sauntered ahead, not knowing that Nayan had stopped. Nayan chose a bright red vermillion casket and inquired its price.

'Fifteen rupees, beta,' the old woman said. The girl took the casket, opened its lid and began filling it with a fistful of red powder she picked from a little mound of vermillion, her blind gaze turned upwards towards the sky.

'You look very beautiful today. Getting married, beta?' asked the old woman, putting out her hand eagerly, to feel the silk of Nayan's sari.

'Yes,' Nayan answered. Jeeban had come back to the stall and stood watching.

'God bless you, my child,' the old woman said, smiling so that the gaps between her broken teeth showed. She asked her granddaughter to wish Nayan happiness. The blind girl gave Nayan the casket, leaned forward and gave Nayan a hug. Nayan was speechless. Tears filled her eyes. As they walked away, Nayan turned back to look at the blind girl again. She was smiling, her face turned towards the burnished orange expanse of the sky. The old woman was still mouthing blessings after them.

By the time they reached the ghat, preparations for the Ganga aarti were in full swing. The river stretched from below the flight of stone steps to the other bank, beyond which lay stark spreads of white silt. The water heaving at the edges of the steps on the stony bank appeared a dirty mossy green.

The ghat was abuzz with a confused mélange of onlookers. A few metres away from Jeeban stood a loud-mouthed tourist guide speaking to a group of white tourists. 'Now we will all see how this group of five young pundits perform the evening aarti puja to appease the river goddess, our own Ganga Maiyya!'

'Meera would have loved to paint here,' Jeeban said, panning the place with his gaze.

Nayan nodded. 'She would have…'

She thought of her mother then. Ratri usually sat down at this time with her tanpura to sing. What would she sing today? Puriya Dhanashri? What should she sing today while her daughter is about to get married? Raga Durga maybe? After finishing riyaz, she will call out to Rani to give her instructions for dinner. She thought about her father. He must be in his study with a black tumbler of tea by his side, books piled up all over his desk. And Neel, he would be travelling with Gehna in to Kerala where they had been shooting with Palash Mitra for the past few months. Everything would happen as per routine while she was about to marry Jeeban. No one knew she was going to get married.

The Ganga aarti began. Five young, self-confident priests

came and stood with their heads held high on the bank facing the river and blew conch shells together. Then, lighting up fifty-one wicks in each of their colossal copper lamps, they began swaying them before the river to the soulful hymns of the choir seated under a dome on a circular extension of the ghat. From a distance, the singers appeared to be sitting in the middle of the river.

Handing the vermillion casket to Jeeban, Nayan walked past the priests to the edge of the ghat. She joined the many women there who were lighting small earthen lamps lined up on the steps that descended into the river. Nayan picked up a candle. As she tilted the candle to light the oil-soaked wicks, hot wax dripped down to her fingers.

'Isn't love about losing oneself, annihilating oneself? Love is not love if it does not consume the lover in its fire. Like a candle flame devours the candle itself, reduces it to formless wax, love must consume to sustain itself. Love must take its toll to let love reign supreme, to let its idea live on in people's hearts,' Salil had read out from a book once, while they sat in his studio after making love. She had felt light as a moth in summertime, the air in his studio lifting her up like she were something made of feathers. Salil's hands knew by heart the story of her body. He mapped with his fingers on her palms new paths of pleasure. It always felt like the joints in their bodies, all their bones had been designed for each other, to fit into each other's crooks perfectly. In the world outside the studio, their bodies were like the pieces of some jigsaw puzzle, either all over the place or excruciatingly shy and shrunken in their own shells. But, when they were near each other, they seemed to come together in a magical communion. Her hands and feet felt like water, flowing from one end of the day to the other with him. Her breathing became easy, like some underwater creature blowing bubbles in the deep seas.

Chants rose from a crowd of onlookers. The hymns picked up a little pace. The five priests turned in all four directions, swaying their copper lamps to and fro in the air. Nayan sat down on the first step going down to the river. The water reflected the hypnotic swing of the flames. The divine assembly turned fluid with religious fervour. Spectres from the past and present flew like sparks around her.

'It's the Bagmati – witness to my love, my life – that has come bursting out, ripping apart my nerves, and scattering away, flooding, submerging my immediate reality... This house that I live in as the new bride from Nepal...' Nayan noticed the river turn ashen. The breeze grew cold. Her hair stood on end. She looked at the woman sitting next to her. The woman turned to face Nayan, and they exchanged glances. Nayan had no idea what Gehna's mother looked like, but she froze at the certainty that this woman next to her was Maithili.

The flames continued to pendulate in an opiate rhythm, like the pipe of a snake charmer. Nayan started feeling delirious. A multitude of prayers poured from every voice on the bank.

In their midst she heard her own voice, too: 'You know, Salil, Jeeban, the stubborn, kurta-clad, bearded, live-life-king-size bloke, and Meera, the painter, are due to get married by Diwali this year. Isn't it lovely? They are in love, Jeeban and Meera...' She heard Jugnu whisper into her ears: 'Those years have flown past, Nayan. Life seems to have forgotten innocence. It seems to have made a remote memory of everything... we grew up believing as our own...' Tears rolled down Nayan's cheeks. She felt faint and tried to find something to hold on to. She looked around anxiously for Jeeban, but he seemed to be lost in the crowd. She felt dizzy. Scared of falling down the steps into the river, she tried to step back and the loose end of her sari caught in something, a nail jutting out of a wooden chouki on which the women sat perhaps. She could not tell one thing from the other. The flames from the aarti, their reflections in the dark river – one thing merged into the other. The bells in the surrounding temples were clanging ceaselessly. The site transformed into a wilderness of searching voices. Nayan pulled her sari to free herself and it tore. Her throat was parched. She needed someone to hold her.

Maithili's voice echoed from across time and space in her ears:

'But, I know, I know like hell that this world shall swell up and turn so vast now that I shall never see him again. That man in Maddox Square, and I, will get lost in this big wide world, and not meet ever.'

A few enthusiatic tourists and saffron-clad men and women began to dance, their flowing robes swirling, their saris and shirts billowing in the air. Nayan sagged like a heap of old clothes on the floor, calling out to Jugnu. She pleaded with her in her withering voice, but instead the writer returned from the dead to her.

> 'I have outgrown my long-preserved sanity
> lime-green geckos of madness
> speak all day long
> through the cracks in the mask now
> I see wild tails of gross detachment
> Dance tirelessly
> Swirl cruelly
> To a silent ballad in my heart'

Some disc-shaped bronze gongs were sounded. The frenzied devotion that had energized the whole gathering moments ago slowly lulled to an unprecedented restfulness. The priests put down the dwindling lamps and prostrated themselves before the river goddess.

Nayan stood up, crying hysterically. She walked down the flight of steps and sat on the last step but one. Her sari got wet near her ankles as the river water heaved around her feet. The crowd began to disperse and Jeeban found his way down the ghat. He sat beside her. Little girls and boys ran down the steps and released tiny earthen lamps in lotus leaves on the water. After making sure their lamps were floating steadily, they ran back up the steps past Jeeban and Nayan. It was eight o'clock. Jeeban checked his watch. The past hour had made such a difference to him. He was feeling lighter, strangely unburdened after so many days. The tears that had rained on Nayan's face dried up, leaving stains of salty water. She sat looking at the river.

Half an hour went by. The ghat was quiet, except for the kirtan singers who could be heard somewhere in the distance, and a few children who ran down the steps to float their earthen lamps in the river.

Around the time they were supposed to walk to the small temple where the pundit would get them married, Nayan looked at Jeeban. Her decision glimmered calm and clear in her eyes. Jeeban knew what it was. The burden on them, the clot of stagnated air between them had dissolved. Jeeban stood up and walked down the remaining steps that plunged into the river, those one couldn't see but only feel with one's feet. He bent down and released the casket of vermillion in the water.

Then he came back and sat beside Nayan. They sat watching the river for hours they did not count. The earthen lamps drifted away till they looked like tiny sequins embracing the oblivion.

Now I understand

She looked every bit like Sameera. Except her eyes. Those were Firoz's eyes. A faint greyish-blue, slightly cold, like a doll's. Salil's mother had once bought Sameera a blue-eyed doll from Kolkata that fluttered her eyelashes coquettishly when moved. Moving about the house, she looked inside and at everything, from old chests to closets to the attic. She asked for locked drawers to be unlocked. She removed books from the shelves in her grandfather's study to search for secret vaults. She would talk to plants for hours together in the kitchen garden, pick a dry leaf or two while walking down the road, place it on her palm and look at it with a deep sense of involvement. Her innocence was both beautiful and profound. It amazed Salil that a child her age could have a clearly defined personality, that she walked about as if she were on her own, weaving her own stories, thinking her own thoughts, writing her own secret life in her mind. Everyone had a hidden world within that did

When my worlds
wake up rubbing
their sleepy eyes from
a long magical sleep,
You & I will have
grown old in our
hollow worlds...

not show up on their faces. How picturesque or ugly depended really on how exquisitely or grotesquely your DNA lay coiled up inside you; it all connected up to science after all. This kid had delicately spiced twists of genes that suited her perfectly.

Sameera came to India after eight years with her six-year-old daughter Sadia. Her husband Firoz was expected to come down in two weeks' time to meet her parents and to take Sameera and Sadia back home. It was after very long that all four in the family sat together at lunch, munched crispies over tea and relived old days at dinner. Salil's mum, dad, Sameera and Salil. They were together again, doting over little Sadia all the time. Sameera had changed in many ways. Streaks of Zahida, someone Salil had only tried to imagine at times, were apparent in his sister although she tried very hard to be the person she had been at home years ago. Every afternoon, as they lay together in bed after lunch, their mother asked Sameera questions about the goings-on in a Muslim household, wanting to know how things were in Firoz's family. This was the closest she could get to knowing their culture. Each one tried to avoid any kind of bitterness, convincing oneself that bygones were bygones now that so many years had passed. Moreover, Sameera was happy and that was reason enough to do away with the hurt of her famous rebellion.

Salil had come home specially to be with his sister. He had been busy with writing. He lived mostly with Raghu in Saharanpur when not travelling. That apart, he also stayed for many months in Corbett inside the forest where Raghu's elder brother was posted as a forest conservator. Raghu had recently married a girl who worked in his aunt's school. Salil had decided to leave the newly-weds alone and travel elsewhere when he heard Sameera was coming down. He did go to Delhi sometimes, stopped over at friends', or lived alone in empty rooms that people let out. He bumped into people who knew her – her college mates, her friends from music school – but never into her. It had been so long now. Almost three years. And nothing to show for all these years of not meeting her. He had never really analysed what had gone wrong. He just knew he couldn't take her goodness and her placidity. Their relationship was either too pure to be sullied, too fragile to handle, or it was something to do with Nayan. The illusion that he knew and understood her didn't hold because he knew no one could know anyone completely. And Nayan, never. For she had something like an invisible city inside her mind, her own separate realm of everything she was. Her deep quietude that lent her a kind of inscrutability was too private to be encroached on in any way. Salil believed it would be a crime to do that. He knew her well enough to know she needed to be left alone. That was reason enough for him to stay away. These were abstract things, reasons difficult to explain to anyone other than one's own self.

He had a blurry justification for breaking away, leaving alone his own restlessness, which he always counted in as one of the reasons. He knew of her decision to marry Jeeban. That was over two-and-a-half years ago. A common friend of Jeeban's had told him. Envy was a thing alien to him. He was not jealous, nor was he angry with Nayan or Jeeban. Just a little lonelier than before. But he was meant to carry on with life like that, aimlessly as before. His books were being appreciated now. Maybe he needed to do just that, write.

In Sadia, he thought, there was this intense aloofness that reminded him of Nayan. 'What colour is aloofness?' Nayan had asked one afternoon while they were painting his studio walls. 'Your colour!' he had replied. 'Then I must be my dad's colour! He's the most aloof person I have ever known.'

Sadia also asked such questions. 'Uncle, why are these clouds so dark? Are they always upset? Or, are they always angry?' Looking at a sapphire Salil's mother wore on her ring finger, she asked, 'Nani, why do you wear the sea on your finger? Can anybody own the seas?'

But Mum said all children ask questions out of curiosity. Sameera was never like this. She was an uncomplicated go-getter, with a practical approach towards everything in life, including love. That was why, once in love, she went ahead and married Firoz against Mum and Dad's wishes, without wasting much time mulling over the idea. To her a compromise or a decision came very quickly, as though to meet certain deadlines in life. She was everything Salil wasn't.

Salil did not know Firoz so he wasn't sure how much Sadia had taken after her father. But he thought Sadia was also a lot like him. Her remoteness bore a semblance to his at least. Laws of inheritance, they worked.

He loved the little girl. He spent hours walking with Sadia, showing her places, telling her stories, taking her to his favourite bakery to buy her stick jaw.

Sadia kept a diary which she was very possessive about. She kept scribbling little nothings, pasting pictures inside. She wrote about the plants she spoke to. At the age of seven, she had a personality of her own. She slipped into bouts of silence sometimes, hiding in some corner of the house, under some table, or inside the bathtub. Or else, she would slip inside a tent she made by tying Salil's mother's sari to four chairs and pretend to be out on a jungle safari.

The household was young again, fussing over Sadia, adoring her antics. A little girl had changed their lives, and bewildered Salil. She played games with Salil. She commanded him to set up hospitals on flower pots for the injured ants and sick butterflies that she would get on stretchers made out of dry leaves stapled on flat matchsticks. If there were not many ants and butterflies who needed help, she would stamp her foot lightly on some of the ants and drag them to her court. She would admit them into separate rooms and wards, which were rectangles and squares etched on wet mud with toothpicks. Then she would treat them by daubing Boroline on a broken leg, talcum powder and coconut oil on a broken wing, and talk about them as 'That patient from room no. 3, he should get well soon.' Those which died would be given solemn funerals, and being the oldest in the household, Salil's dad had no choice but to play the priest and get the burial done outside in the lawn.

One day while Salil sat reading in a green nook behind his house, Sadia came up to him.

'Goodmorning, Uncle!'

'Morning, li'l one. So what's the game for today?' he asked.

'Today…' She thought a little and said, 'Yes, today I'm the pink princess trapped in my ivory tower. You, I command, shall be the court magician! But what will your name be? Umm?'

She thought and said, 'Yes. Tinterpank! That's your name. So that's what we will play today, Tinterpank. You understand?'

'Yes, your Highness,' answered Salil.

'And Nana will be the cruel king, my father, Crownman. And Nani will play the witch – Lymanta. And, Mum will play my prince!'

Salil smiled. 'So we're in for an action-packed day, eh?'

Sadia placed both her hands on her waist and nodded.

'So Tinterpank, when Crownman traps me in the ivory tower and Lymanta casts a spell on my prince, Casper, you will have to help me. You will give him the invisible letter I write to him. That invisible letter, nobody shall see. Only my prince shall know the trick. With the letter's help, he will free himself of Lymanta's dark spell.'

'Yes, Princess. As you wish.' Salil laughed at her Shakespearean concoction.

'Uncle!'

'Yes, little princess?'

'Do you know how to write invisible letters?'

'No, Princess, I'm no magician.'

'This is no magic, Uncle. My teacher taught me how to write them, at school. You write them with orange juice. When it dries up, the paper looks blank. No letter at all! But when my prince passes it over a candle flame, he will be able to see the words. I'll go and ask Nani for some juice and show you how. Stay here. I'll be back.' She dashed inside the house.

Salil got up. He went to his room, pulled his desk drawer open and took out an envelope the size of a little shopping bag. He looked at the reams of blank sheets that fell out onto his desk when he turned the envelope upside down. Then, shaking his head incredulously, he put the sheets back into the envelope with care. A little girl had told him the trick. That was what she had come all the way from England for. He knew now.

The day ended and stars came out in the sky. Sadia's game had ended, the prince had been freed, and now she was fast asleep on the settee in Salil's room. Salil sat at his desk, thinking and playing his mouth organ softly. Outside the window, he could see the mist caught in the pine trees beyond his fence. Around midnight, he picked up the envelope again. Taking out a candle from his drawer, he lit it with his cigarette lighter and pulled out all the blank pages Nayan had given him the last time they had met. Slowly, he passed them over the candle flame, one by one. As the night went by, every word in Nayan's letters woke up as if from a long spell.

Salil read each one of them. So many years had gone by. So much had passed between them since then. But she loved him despite everything. All that she had seen, the people she had written to him about, told him she knew how to love, and better than him.

'When my words wake up
rubbing their bleary eyes

from a long magical sleep,
You and I will have
grown old in
our hollow worlds…'

The last of the letters trailed to a slow silence. He picked up a rucksack, and stuffed it with some clothes. Then, gathering all the letters, he walked out of the house in the direction of the bus station. If not the last one tonight, he would surely catch the first bus to Delhi before dawn.

Acknowledgements

My parents, because they believe there is space in this world for someone like me.

Arshia Sattar, D.W. Gibson and Prof. Laurie Patton, for giving me the gift of time at Sangam House, Nrityagram.

At HarperCollins: Shuka and Arijit, for arranging the charming illustrations and the beautiful cover; Shantanu, for his editorial insights; and Karthika, for seeing this impossible book through.

My saner half, my best and worst critic, Indrajit: can't thank you enough for being there, no matter what.

Thank you all very, very much.